Looking for Lakshmi

RAJAN SONI

UNISA PRESS
PRETORIA

For my daughters, Radha and Aditi

And in memory of my father, Rajinder Pal Soni

© 2015 University of South Africa
First edition, first impression

ISBN 978-1-86888-794-1

Published by Unisa Press
University of South Africa
P O Box 392, 0003 UNISA

Prior to acceptance for publication by Unisa Press, this work was subjected to a double-blind peer review process mediated through the Senate Publications Committee of the University of South Africa.

Project Editor: Alicia de Wet
Copy-editor: Alexandra Dodd
Book design and typesetting: Thea Bester-Swanepoel
Printer: Lebone Litho Printers (Pty) Ltd
Cover image: Rectangular cloth, 26 x 35 cm, with the symbol for Om embroided in the centre. Photograher: Jasmine Parker; supplied by author
Text Om image: © Katyau, Shutterstock
Cover background image: © Allies Interactive, Shutterstock

Telephone: 086 12 DALRO (from within South Africa); +27 (0)11 712-8000
Telefax: +27 (0)11 403-9094
Postal Address: P O Box 31627, Braamfontein, 2017, South Africa
www.dalro.co.za

Every effort has been made to trace copyright holders or use works in the public domain. We apologise for any inadvertent omissions, and will correct such errors if pointed out.

Contents

Unisa Flame Series
Foreword

THE UNISA FLAME SERIES was sparked by the need to create a space in which to publish groundbreaking works of high merit and originality which move beyond the scope of the traditional.

Manuscripts that point to new expressive pathways, new ways of making sense of our reality, and new kinds of interactive explanation are published here. As original, creative and analytical materials, these manuscripts transcend the boundaries of subject field and medium, and are typically hard to package as either academic or popular. The aim of the Series is thus to open up a space at Unisa Press for new forms of expression which defy classical academic categories of publishing.

Within this paradigm of unlocking the future, which draws on Africa's scrambled periodization in which premodernity, modernity and postmodernity cohabit, the Series draws in works that are cutting-edge and which cater for a new generation of digital natives as well as for an existing print-based readership. As a flagship series, the Unisa Flame Series publishes select prestigious works in any of a range of suitable mediums.

Works in this Series are of a multi-, inter- and trans-disciplinary nature, and come from within a range of academic and professional/ practitioner disciplines.

This fourth book within the Series, *Looking for Lakshmi,* maps a journey of yearning and self-discovery, following a trail of clues to uncover the true identity of Rajan Soni's paternal grandmother, Bibiji. In this process, the author also discovers himself, in an eclectic narrative shaped along the emergent theme of life writing.

This is a highly personal journey, created by eloquently fusing the traditional formats of the memoir and the historical narrative. Tapping into lived experiences, Soni refines his descriptions with accurate, yet lyrical details. Stylistically, this is a complex debut, further enriched with reference to Hindu mythology. Such references are woven into the narrative with accuracy and poise – drawing inspiration from the Ramayana, the Bhagavad Gita, Kabir poetry and from Indological literature generally.

Structured in a complex set of shifting timeframes as the author's memory leaps into different timeframes, the narrative nevertheless establishes a strong central line by integrating the various stories into specific historic landscapes. This voyage of self-discovery is set against the unfolding history of Africa and India, in its transition from colonial to postcolonial – so that the sweeping events swiftly draw readers into the narrative. Evocative and sensual details add to an almost filmic reading experience.

Looking for Lakshmi significantly contributes to the African contemporary literature by adding a unique new slant to the genres of the memoir and travel writing; so that Rajan Soni successfully extends Unisa Press's reach as a publisher of innovative works. Fusing a brave personal narrative with Indian diaspora history and a gender-specific and Africa-specific context , this is a noteworthy debut and proud addition to the Unisa Flame Series.

Keyan G Tomaselli
Alan Weinberg

Acknowledgements

MIGRANTS HAVE TO travel light, carrying only that which is essential for survival and renewal. Papers, photos and books are heavy.

When I began this book my mother, Suraksh Kanta, handed over an astonishing array of material meticulously packaged in polythene folders, which had endured countless migrations across countries and decades: school reports and diaries from childhood and teenage years, official documents and grainy family photographs, memorabilia that spoke of tears in the fabric of family life, and books that I had been attached to in earlier years. But more valuable than all this, was her elephantine, matriarchal memory. This book would have been impossible without her. Thank you, Mama.

My thanks to three of Bibiji's surviving children who allowed me to return time and again, and ask difficult questions: my uncles Krishan Gopal and Vijay Pal, and my aunt Swaran Kanta, who besides answers, always met me with a hug, bed and meal, no matter when I arrived unannounced in Delhi.

And finally, my profound thanks to my editor, Alex Dodd, for her encouragement and empathy through this long journey. We began this journey as professional associates, and emerged as friends. I salute her aesthetic spirit, insightful mind and unforgiving literary eye. She got me here.

Chapter One

I WAS AT SEA when the smell of my ancestors came out to bring me ashore. The blush of tangerine in the morning sky had faded; the mood and colours of the ocean spoke another language. Choppy, brown waves slapped up against the bow of the ship. The sea no longer heaved and swelled as it had done mid-ocean under the searing equatorial sun. Then it had driven third class passengers down into the bowels of the SS *Karanja*, bending adults into foetal positions on bedrolls scattered in the metallic shade.

Most days, in the heat of the early afternoon, I would retreat to my windowless cabin. The toothless old Gujarati man, who had laid claim to the bottom bunk closest to the door, had pulled the stained spittoon even closer, within retching distance of his pillow. I would lie on the far top bunk and look down on him through my own nausea, clutching a tired English paperback or the journal that had become my faithful companion during that trip. He would return my stare vacantly. From time to time, he would rise on an elbow, lean towards the receptacle and, with a jerk, add fresh layers to the cocktail of oil, sea and human odour that filled the submarine compartment occupied by eight men.

In 12 days at sea, he had spoken to me only once.

'You Punjabi?' he had asked in Gujarati soon after we set sail.

'*Ji ha.*' Yes, sir, I had replied in Hindi.

He had nodded, not unkindly.

I was relieved that he did not speak to me again. At 18, cooped in a cubicle with a group of middle-aged Indian men, I may well have been asked to shift the spittoon. Their claim to respect as elders would have overridden the lines of language, caste and religion, which criss-crossed that cabin. I can only assume that it was the books I carried with me and the scribbles in my diary that saved me.

The innards of the ship had begun to stir well before dawn that February morning in 1972 when the sticky past came to meet me. By five in the morning, the third-class ablution facilities were already sloshy, a whiff of the three months of Indian train and station loos to come. When I ascended the steep metal stairs to the open deck, there was a silent crowd on the right side of the bow. Widespread arms gripped the handrail, reserving space for family members left below to pack trunks and tie bedrolls. Faces were turned to the east, scouring the horizon towards which we had been sailing for days. Around us, the crew moved with a new purposeful haste, loosening thick coils of briny, greying rope and clanging long blades of rusting levers.

Though the waters were calm, the faces around me bore a fateful strain. Young eyes searched for signs of land, their gazes trained by the family stories that had called them back from Africa. Older eyes, clouded by the shadows of bittersweet memories, squinted into the spray of the salty present. Seagulls arced past, then down to find angular protrusions and hanging rafts.

The breeze began to thicken with a smell that had first floated into my awareness as a child. I remember that smell emerging from the large tin trunk that we gathered around whenever my maternal grandfather, Bauji, returned from India. The extended family would sit cross-legged on the polished cement floor after the evening prayers. The day's reunions completed, Bauji would swing open the lid of the trunk and a cloying cloud would slowly fill the room. It was that same rich, tangy, earthy, sweet smell that seemed permanently attached to the cottons and bodies of older people, and to anyone who came from India: visiting swamis in wooden clogs, chance sailors from the ancestral village brought home unannounced by my father or uncles for dinner, relatives and neighbours who returned with louder voices, and fingers that had learnt to pinch our cheeks more painfully in greeting.

I would watch the trunk intently to see exactly where this smell came from. Bauji would shift his large frame forward and pull out packets of Afghani pine nuts, Kashmiri saffron and Punjabi jaggery; hockey sticks and *gilli-danda* sets for the boys, *chunnis* and bright bangles for the girls; Mysorian incense and pictures of avatars for the *puja* room. Then, as the gifts carried away the attention of their recipients, I would reach in to explore the trunk, hands drifting past coarse *khaddar* and thick *dhurries*, finding the odd glass marble and loose drops of sugared aniseed. But my searching eyes could never find the source of the smell that seeped into my bones.

And here it was; deeper and fuller, thick and putrid – the smell of ancestors.

My father never talked about his mother.

One day, a blue-edged envelope came, with a garland of small stamps splayed in the right corner – brown and green portraits of the bespectacled Gandhiji. I was eight and alert to any signs that might portend turmoil in my parents or between them.

Letters with the Mahatma's image presaged conflict in the house. His toothy smile invariably brought news and demands from India that sullied the innocence of the new family my parents were creating in Mombasa. Names and claims would fly off a page and stir buried memories and passions. Too often, the ink of India would colour our meals. Father's face would tighten, his voice rise, and he would stay away from the kitchen where he would otherwise have been helping to peel the vegetables. Mama would cook alone, her face the red of a ripe, bruised tomato, lined and twisted with the bitterness of a *karela*. She would place his food on the table, retreat to the clammy plastic sofa in the front room, and cry. I would ache, not knowing who to eat with. It wouldn't matter anyway; the shadows in the house would grip my throat.

When they raged, their colliding stories would twist and grow larger, deepening the wounds they brought to the next fight. I would coil into myself. I'd go up to the roof terrace of the house, lie on a grass mat and listen to the stars, my mother's and father's voices echoing inside me. The sea breeze would sing softly through the mango and jamun trees, and play on my bare arms, legs and face.

Lying there, I sensed a dissonance I could not name then, but which, in time, would threaten to drive me away from the community into which I was born, and then later still, pull me back with an unexpected intensity. I sensed that my family's history seethed with stories of hurt – and that these stories had limitless vibrancy and endurance, and that if I remained in their presence they would tear and transfigure me as they did all adults.

My parents' stories usually returned to the same characters. The theme too stayed much the same: my father's unflinching resolve to send money to India to support his siblings, and my mother's demand that this should stop someday. I would listen to their rows, far enough away not to be consumed by their fire, close enough to catch the embers and carry them to the next generation. My large, protruding ears sought out the underlying threads, pausing unsure over the names of people I had never seen. It was easy to smell my parents' prejudices; the odour oozed off the bare walls whitewashed by the involuntary expletives and pauses that went with a name.

Most weekends I would accompany my father to the post office. We would walk past the leafy rubber trees in Treasury Square to the tall cream columns of the post office building. I would run down the veranda lined with small grey hatches, each neatly numbered one less than the one before, to come to a stop before 547. Father would smile. He expected numerical exactness from me, and could never resist immediate celebration.

'Shah-baassh', he would say, that rolling, petering sound so much sweeter and more pregnant with promise than the pointedness of 'well done'. But the light and lines on his face could change quickly as he withdrew the mail from the box.

The day that letter came his face furrowed immediately, spiked by the energy of ancient ley lines of the heart. He read the letter in my mother's presence, his eyes moving slowly from right to left as he deciphered the Urdu script. My mother's agitation was plain, but different from anything I had heard before, as if she were struggling between respect and fear. Her tone of voice was mostly soft, occasionally hardening to a jagged edge. Her words suggested alarm, duty, expectation and anxiety, and it was as if she were afraid that someone was listening.

'Is Bapu really coming? When is he coming? He will be staying with us? How long will he stay with us? Who's paying for Bapu's ticket?'

Father's voice – which, like my mother's, had fluency, range and a clarity that made them both essential chorus leaders of the evening *aarti* at the temple – gave way to a throaty joviality. That was how he spoke when he was tense.

'Yes, he's coming. Where else would he be staying? With the neighbours?'

I don't remember who he said would be paying for the ticket. It was the kind of question my mother would always ask. By then I was not listening to their words. My ears had closed before the omens of the lost meals to come.

Bapu, my paternal grandfather arrived three months later. He was a rugged man, with watchful eyes. As a conversation moved, his steady gaze could drift or settle directly, offering a ready space for conflict. There was an unkempt insouciance and an upright angularity about him.

His gait, curiosity and manner of speech revealed that he was out of his element on the coral sands of the Swahili coast. But this did not lend him an air of vulnerability, or make him overly tender. Throughout his time with us, he retained a confident smile and a casual severity that suggested unbending independence. He wore white shirts and loose, creamy cotton *kurta*-pyjamas. All other items of clothing – trousers, jackets and shawls – were in hues of brown and grey, the colours of dirt and earth from a distant land.

Up to then, perhaps even more so than my own parents, the centre of my familial universe had been my maternal grandmother, Wadimama, as I called her. Her scent, songs and charisma had filled my world from birth, and I found the certainty of love in the folds of her soft sari, sitting beside her for evening prayers at the temple most evenings.

It was she who had brought me up from infancy, and accompanying her through the day, I saw the world revolving around Wadimama and my maternal grandfather. In that household were my mother's five brothers, and beyond them, an extended family of uncles and cousins and assorted other relatives and village kin who had given my parents a start in Mombasa. This was the Nayar clan. I had grown up in their luxuriant shade. But sometimes, just sometimes, I felt an element of unease that, despite being absolutely accepted by this family, I was not wholly a chip off their block. Perhaps this sense of separateness was evolutionary – childhood giving way to individual consciousness. Or maybe there is in us an ageless self, a 'silent witness', which is wiser beyond our years. Whatever its origin, this sense of apartness felt intimately real and disturbing, physically and spiritually.

Bapu's arrival cut into this closed world.

His bony face, big ears, lean frame and jutting chin were a mirror that framed some nagging, but also oddly affirming, questions. I would gawk at him, held by the discernable resemblance in his and my father's features. He would look back, with a dry, conspiratorial smile. The traces of biology did not stop there. I saw similar contours etched into the geography of my own face and body.

But more than anything else, it was the unexpected mores that he provoked in our house, which broadened and disturbed the certainties with which I had grown up. For the time that Bapu was with us, my father went for a walk with his father, not me. I saw my mother more hospitable and energetic than ever before – hurrying into the kitchen as soon as she returned from work, relentlessly looking for different vegetables to cook, or the same seasonal ones to be prepared in different ways. There was more butter in the food, and the house crackled with her agitated, dutiful hospitality, like a *puja*-fire spitting with excess *ghee*. I would catch her hiss in private, but in public, mother would be utterly deferential to Bapu; and before going to bed, she would unfailingly put a long steel tumbler of hot milk by his bedroom door.

Most evenings, Bapu steered the conversation to those universal motifs burnished by visitors when the sun is setting in a foreign land – the call of blood and clan, outstanding courtesies and buried wounds, memories of siblings and elders, neighbours and soil. Bapu would begin, his voice thick and gravely, knobbly like the bark of an old mango tree, rich with fruit. The distinct dark strains in his speech would draw me in from the sandy fields and roof terraces where we played. I would listen, ensnared by the twilight and stilled by the foreboding of a black-and-white Dilip Kumar tragedy. My mind would wander as I sought to transpose this new grandfather into familiar locales from my childhood, but I could never imagine him singing in the temple, or serving food at a communal feast.

He spoke a crude Punjabi, the kind I came to miss after my father died twenty-eight years later. But whereas my father's words would mellow with age, and sparkle even more with the poetry of Kabir, Bapu's language was seasoned with the Urdu anvils of customary law: *izzat, farz, hukam* and *jaat* – honour, duty, absolute authority and clan.

He would pound and twist old stories and reshape them with a troubling air of nonchalance. The retreating limits of my vocabulary would struggle to keep pace with the shifting cameos carved by his jagged idioms, his strong eyes deep with the shadows of ancestors. The effect would jangle me.

Always he returned to the land. Ancestral land, productive, invaluable land – land that rightfully belonged to the family and was now lost. Each time the subject came up, father's pupils would shimmer with a light that offered no truck to ghosts and shadows of yore. He would either laugh and turn away, or say, 'Let it go; let's not talk about our land.'

One day, as Bapu teased out another story buried in their shared past, he pushed on, disregarding father's plea. I suspected, from the intonation in his voice, that he did this wilfully. My mother withdrew quickly. A sudden fury consumed my father. His face quivered as he turned to Bapu directly. There was a smouldering edge in his voice that came very seldom, but when it did we knew not to confront it. In the words that followed I heard him say, 'Bibiji died because of that land...'

His body shook as he struggled to contain a wild fire. That word, 'Bibiji', stood out, an island of inviolability in the flames that threatened to engulf the house. Bapu stood his ground, his stare inviting conflict; his lips chose silence.

That night, as I rubbed the soles of my feet against the coarse, breeze-block wall by my bed to call forth sleep, I heard my parents talking softly, intimately, in the room next door. I was on the far edge of their conversation. That same word appeared unpredictably like a full moon glimpsed through a bank of racing clouds. Each time my father said, 'Bibiji', it was imbued with respect and tenderness, as if he were touched by the stillness of a silver night.

Bapu did not remain long with us. He went after three weeks, to stay 'up-country' with my father's younger brother, who my parents had supported through medical school. We said goodbye to him at the railway station, standing by the bunked, male compartments for Indians. A few whites walked past to their first-class cabins beyond the restaurant coach, at the flower-bedded end of the platform. Bapu did not even steal a look at them. My mother's bright, darting eyes pointed to the food she had packed for him. My father chuckled and swung my three-year-old brother onto his shoulders, offering his favourite son's handsome face to a wider horizon. Bapu ruffled my hair and leant forward to plant words into my floppy ears, which had come from him. 'Son, you are my eldest grandson. You carry our name.'

His prominent chin filled the canvas. His tenor was gruff and insistent – so unlike my father's light, versatile voice that could easily break into laughter, whistling and song; a trait that my brother would inherit. It was a moment like many others that would follow as I grew older, lit by an awareness of the vagaries and unreturnable gifts of inheritance. What had been bequeathed to me, and by whom? I looked away from Bapu, seeking redemption from an ungainly lineage. Another figure beckoned. A woman – nameless, faceless and wielding a power that becalmed my father into a profound and unexplained silence.

That dim vision of Bibiji bestirred by Bapu would take years to mature. It would develop slowly in my psyche for nearly half a century before sharpening into a quest that would take me to India in 2005 to trace Bibiji's life. In the intervening years, her enigma would be sustained by chance anecdotes and epiphanies. Each incident would add to my sense of frustration about her invisibility in the family annals. Never once in those decades would I hear Bibiji's story recounted as a woman in her own right, an ancestor worthy of appreciation.

In time, I would look back and see two streams taking me to the riverbank where her ashes were poured into the Ganges. There was the curiosity about my father's abiding silence regarding his mother, who had died seven years before I was born. And there was the ferment of my variegated self – formed on an island of communalism and fragmented with the force of Independence and relentless migrations.

The river would sally with its own questions. Was this compulsion to understand the play of destiny and history that had shaped my life, Bibiji's bequest – her restive genes carrying me back to her?

I first saw Bibiji's blurred ghost when Bapu came and went in 1961.

My eyes were playing tricks. Everywhere I turned the colours and shapes of childhood were shifting, transmuting. Things and events were accruing new names, meanings and associations. In those hazy times, as I edged my way to the front row to be near the teacher's blackboard or below the towering drive-in screen, the voices I heard didn't just become louder and the images less fuzzy; the stories themselves changed.

Within two years, in 1963 at the age of ten, I was wearing spectacles. In those two years Bibiji's spectre hardly moved, imprisoned in the shadows of our family life. The light, meanwhile, was falling brightly on emblems of freedom. Mombasa was awash with green, black and red streamers stamped with black shields and crossed spears. Kenya raised its own flag on 12 December 1963. That December we followed the new Kenyan flag to its source in the capital, Nairobi.

It was a predictable pilgrimage, looking back, not forward – supposedly apolitical, yet perversely political. We went, as was our tradition, to vacation with my father's eldest sister, Savitri Bua.

Bibiji's first child was a girl, who died at two. Savitri followed, and survived infancy to grow into a girl destined to lead Bibiji's brood of nine children into adulthood. As Bibiji's eldest daughter, she had served the longest apprenticeship in her mother's increasingly impoverished house.

Savitri Bua was a large, emotional woman whose aphorisms, mantras, books and absent afternoons revealed an unswerving dedication to the Arya Samaj. This was the reformist Hindu movement that had contributed more than three quarters of the men hanged by the British in the Indian nationalist struggle. Her devotion to the Arya Samaj was a passion that had been absorbed from her mother. Bibiji had pioneered the establishment of a group in her own matrimonial village in Punjab, and had sung defiantly of being 'a widow of the martyrs' as she washed the family's laundry by the bleached grey, stone-walled well in the inner courtyard.

The hours after lunch and before tea were the only time Savitri left the house, to lead proceedings at the Arya Samaj woman's group that she had founded in Nairobi. Otherwise, she was wholly present to our visit, embracing us with a hospitality that was occasionally strict, but unfailingly fair. I felt utterly safe in her presence; that surety that a child constructs from a sly reading of infinitesimally small and varied gestures, honed through the lens of sibling rivalries and alertness to petty, surreptitious favours that belie the mannered evenness of extended families. At meal times she would sit us in a line, my brother and I between her sons; cousins alternating in a row, fitting us scrupulously within the chronology of her own family and watching closely to ensure that no one child received a morsel more than any other. That too, I would see, had come from Bibiji.

Savitri had six children, all of whom were unnervingly deferential when their father entered the room. Grown-ups referred to my uncle by his surname, Chopra-ji. It was said as if it had been written in bold. Then in a softer, stretched, italicised tone came his profession: 'a CID'. Everyone seemed to know that he was special. He worked as an investigative policeman with 'Angrez sahibs': English officers at the white core of the colonial service.

He was a Napoleonic man; small, lean, upright, and thin-moustached. We knew little of what he did. He would come home in the early evening in a swirl of curves, the wheels of his black Vanguard spinning under bloated arches, kicking up red highland dust that settled on the looping rear boot of the car. He would alight sprightly, with a smile, as if he expected to be saluted. In the evenings, he sat in a rocking chair with a newspaper – like a 'daddy' in an Enid Blyton story – with Barney, his beloved sausage dog, at his feet. I believed then that his was the only rocking chair and pet dog in the entire Indian universe.

During that stay, Savitri Bua revealed – in an uncharacteristically hushed tone in case any Kikuyu worker was within hearing distance on the other side of the wall of the open courtyard where we ate –

that Chopra-ji had dealt with several murders of 'white women slaughtered by the Mau-Mau'. Now that the perpetrators were in power, the Chopras were emigrating. They would be leaving for India. The expressions on my cousins' faces fluctuated between bewilderment and disappointment.

It was to become a familiar conclusion in the months and years that followed: children of Africa uprooted by adults skulking back to a distant memory of home; congregations leaving behind faraway liberation hymns and hypnotic chants, which would peter and die ritualistically around the singeing fires of racial divisions in East Africa.

A few days after this declaration came the adult ritual that Savitri Bua directed every vacation, in which she always played the lead role. As children, we were both fascinated and frightened by this yearly drama, a loud cathartic row during which the elders raked through family and personal archives to reveal buried claims and disputed legacies. That year the event had a deeper motivation. Savitri Bua was determined to unearth an incontestable edict before leaving the country.

She invited all her siblings and their families. My father had an elder and a younger brother in Kenya then. She cooked from morning to night, and when everyone had eaten, she began railing back and forth over time, until finally she hit the right chord. All the adults began to talk at the same time. Savitri Bua wept between proclamations; an older uncle shouted in protest, his wife screamed and said she was leaving to go home, to 'burn all family photographs'. A younger uncle implored everyone to be calmer in a straining, hopelessly prescriptive voice. My father kept saying, 'Enough. Stop it. I don't want to talk about it now – not here.'

That year, the underlying pattern to these hysterics became apparent. Savitri Bua was obsessed with a figure I couldn't see and my father never named. Her anguish came from a deep source. She saw herself burdened with the unfulfilled vision of a mother who had died too early.

Bibiji's consuming dream had been to see her children educated. Every possible resource at the family's disposal had to be put to that purpose. Savitri Bua invoked matriarchal memory, familial responsibility and sibling duty. She demanded further sacrifice from her brothers. She wanted the three brothers assembled there – and equally importantly their respective wives – to recommit to Bibiji's dream by extending their fraternal covenants to those left behind.

Savitri Bua's hysterics brought Bibiji's ghost closer to the tragicomedy of my parents' marriage. Theirs was a turbulent relationship fraught with polarities: democratic yet solidly traditional; picnics and prayer sessions of joy, followed by terrible conflagrations of jealousy provoked by my father's roving eye and my mother's inherent insecurities. Through it all, the absence of any evidence of infidelities, their warm banter, and the way they shared domestic duties, suggested that my father unfailingly treated my mother as an equal in all but one respect. It was this exception that provoked the explosions, which periodically undermined their harmony.

For the first six years of their marriage, all of my mother's salary, and between a third and half of my father's wage, went directly to India to pay for the education of my father's brothers – first one, and then another. Bibiji's name had never featured in the fiery rows between my parents, sparked by this inviolable tax on their earnings. I began to see that the recurring conflict in their marriage stemmed from an injunction associated with father's mother. Yet I have no memory of any gesture of disrespect by my mother with regard to her. If anything, at the limits of her pain, my mother would compare herself to Bibiji.

It added to the mystery of the woman I could never meet, but whose legacy seemed to play forever through our lives, and whose name I would discover, in a reverential whisper, through my mother.

A *dahdee* without a face
A father who kept no trace
And when the picture came
The two were same-same

Throughout my childhood there was one intellectual exercise in which my father would accept no compromises – juggling numbers through quick additions and subtractions, and memorising multiplication tables. That was the only study time during which he sat with me. It was a discipline he would also impose on my brother and sister when they reached the same age.

I would itch bodily and mentally for what seemed hours as we scrambled in and out of arithmetic solutions and sequences.

7 x 9? *63*
8 x 8? *64*
9 x 9? *81*

By the age of ten my mind had learnt the underlying pattern of grids. I arrived at the answer as often directly, as by bouncing off the immediate numerical relative. 'Nine times ten is ninety, that's easy. So nine times nine must be... the one that comes before... eighty-one, no?'

'Correct,' my father would affirm.

Sometimes alone, other times with my mother, free from homework, I would open the lower drawers of the cupboard in which family heirlooms were kept. That was a happier task; exploring the loose photos, packets of odd-sized prints and the large, meticulously assembled chronological family albums. I would scan the pictures of close and distant relations, and family friends, locating them on this or that side of the family tree. This side, my mother's, was invariably easier and fuller; the other, my father's, always vexing.

My mother's guidance in these explorations was as precise as a mathematical equation. She would identify the person and define them through the immediate paternal or maternal link to me. It was in this way that I learnt the five words for 'uncle' and five for 'aunt'; and the four titles for the grandparents. We sang them to the same beat as the multiplication tables.

Mahmah, Mahmi:	mother's brother, mother's brother's wife
Masad, Mahsi:	mother's sister's husband, mother's sister
Thaya, Thayi:	father's elder brother, father's elder brother's wife
Chacha, Chachi:	father's younger brother, father's younger brother's wife
Foofad, Bua:	father's sister's husband; father's sister
Nana, Nani:	mother's father, mother's mother
Dahdah, Dahdee:	father's father, father's mother

For me, the song ended with the inflexions of emptiness. I would repeat that final name imperceptibly, *'dah, dee, dahdee'*, with the pointed lucidity of a heart that knew it would never touch the words in flesh.

Yet there was never a mention that one image from the matrix of coordinates was missing, that there was no picture of my paternal grandmother. My father, for all his rigour for accuracy, chose not to acknowledge the unseemliness of this blank space. He avoided the issue with such resolve that I could not consider broaching the subject with him. One day I finally asked mother.

'No we haven't. Your *thayi* had some, but she burnt them. I saw a picture of hers once, in India, when we got married. But I don't think there's any picture of Bibiji anywhere now.'

What began as a persistent child's question later became a mission. It was as if, in holding and repeating the question for four decades, I gave life to the conviction that there had to be an image somewhere. And there was. But at the age of eleven, my mind moved on to other ways of filling the gap.

'What was *dahdee*'s name? What did she look like?'

We were looking at the album in which the prized pictures were framed with quarter-inch, silver coloured, corner sticker-pockets. They were mostly from Parekh's Photographic Studio on Station Road. We went there once a year; my father put on a suit and tie, my mother a new sari, her arms laden with golden bangles and her shiny chiffon blouse brushed by her wedding neck-chain. My younger brother and one-year-old sister wore clothes that mother sewed especially for the occasion. I dressed in shorts, patterned shirt and bulbous, black Bata shoes – the best I then had. Everyone's hair was oiled and combed perfectly into place.

I have that picture in my mind's eye now. Mother looks plump, slightly shy and radiant with the happiness of being encircled by her family. My sister's abiding gentleness is already visible in her baby face. My six-year-old brother's eyes sparkle with intelligence and wit. My gangling frame and mule ears promise difficult teens to come. Father has that slightly detached, cool look that settled on his handsome face when he was quiet and at peace.

'Lakshmi Devi,' mother had replied. 'I'm told she was as fair as your father.'

Lakshmi Devi, Bibiji's name, rang divinely across the landscape.

Something about that name had always agitated my soul. Perhaps I had overhead the words whispered by my parents in the night, or in the filling in of an official form. Here was the revelation that I had legitimate claim to that name, as much as it had on me. I knew the words were sacred. Now they were ancestral too. My dead grandmother had incarnated into a goddess.

Pictures of Lakshmi Devi, the Hindu Goddess of Fortune, embodiment of loveliness, grace and charm, consort of the supreme Lord Vishnu, preserver of the universe, were ubiquitous. They hung prominently in virtually every Hindu kiosk and shop. Lakshmi's image was unavoidable in the homes of my Gujarati school friends. She had a special following among the communities of artisans and traders, merchants and moneylenders from India's west coast, who had followed the spoor of the sun in search of a better life. For over a millennium their progenitors had captured the seasonal diagonals of the Kusi and the Kaskazi, the southerly and the north-easterly monsoons traversing the Arabian Sea and sweeping along the east coast of Africa as far south as Mozambique. Theirs was an untold history written on these waters over more than fifteen centuries, of that other marine 'silk road' – Indian cloth, indigo and spices traded over centuries for African ebony, gold and ivory.

Often the goddess's smiling face would be freshly garlanded with fragrant jasmine or orange marigolds, or her forehead dotted with a touch of vermilion – vibrant signs of daily reverence.

Yet in our house there was no picture of Lakshmi Devi. Icons and statuettes of numerous Hindu avatars made their way onto the family altar and the cement walls of the succession of single rooms and flats in which we lived, but not Lakshmi. She perfectly reflected my grandmother's invisibility.

This jumble of coincidences, omissions and divine reflections gleamed like inviting signposts in the dark, pointing across the ocean of dreams that stretched from Kenya to India.

But that moment of beckoning passed. There were other distractions that kept me from answering Bibiji's call; too many other noises of history being unmade and the present morphing fast into a startling future. The island of Mombasa would die within a handful of years, its timeless circle of sea severed by a gorging causeway. On the mainland, primordial savannahs were becoming industrial estates. Everywhere, the walls of communal ghettos were falling. There were new masters of the realm, and they demanded risqué forms of fealty.

Through the cusp of years that straddled the late 1960s and early 1970s, as I moved from childhood into my teens, the harbingers of these upheavals first came at night. Their bewitching voices arrived in open tipper trucks; Kenya African National Union supporters swaying and ululating to mesmerising chants that we had never heard before. They spilled out from the quarry lorries and danced in the dust outside the Yemeni and Swahili shops over the road from our tenement block.

The certainty of their euphoria brought down the ramparts of our Indian ghetto – communalised minds and spatial boundaries, which owed as much to the parochialism of its residents as to the designs of a colonial and racist state. Through those breaches, new gods entered. Kipchoge Keino, who returned with Olympic Gold and Silver from the rarefied air of Mexico City to complete his grinning victory lap in the municipal stadium where we raced. His radiant smile and the easy familiarity with which he tousled my hair, leaving a deeper imprint than the footsteps I sought to follow. Abebe Bikila, the marathon man from Ethiopia next door, who jubilantly ran barefoot into the Rome Stadium just as freely as we leapt across sandy trenches and thorn bushes. The footballers of Gor Mahia shimmying in fluorescent greens as we howled for goals from the open terraces and popped roasted pumpkin seeds. The wizards, James Ngugi – who became Ngũgĩ wa Thiong'o – and Chinua Achebe, casting spells, which metamorphosed the texture of paper, conjuring the landscape right outside the classroom window; arboreal shapes, earthy smells and fleshy colours filling pages, which, until then, had contained frozen words. And riffing through these years, music from America. Artistes with staid European names magicking into big, bold, black characters: James Brown, Ray Charles, Marvin Gaye, Stevie Wonder, Diana Ross. Their music gushed brazenly out from old transistor radios, driven by horns, tambourines, bass guitars and gospel choirs – utterly different from the sitar-filled melodies of my childhood, utterly addictive, and at home in Africa.

In those testosterone years, as Kenya moved inexorably from independence to Africanisation, the cool of the temple where I had heard oral renditions of the Ramayana gave way to the sounds of Motown, and the political pull of Pan-Africanism and Black Consciousness. My identity was unravelling, and around me the rich tapestry of the Indian community in Kenya was being unstitched forever. Bibiji's call had become very faint and sporadic, and gradually I gave up straining to catch a whisper from across the sea.

There was one exception. I was fourteen and in prison.

The day had begun like most Saturday mornings. I left home before eight in my school uniform, pedalling my way to righteousness. I parked the bicycle at a schoolmate's house in Ganjoni. My begging partner, Jitu, met me there. For the rest of the day we worked as a pair, though each with his own collection tin, gathering coins for that week's charity adopted by Mr Heavens, our English teacher. There was an intense competitiveness to this virtue, knowing which shopkeepers to avoid, where the clink would be soft and silver, and where it would be busy with the drizzle of bronze. There were not many Mondays when my name did not head the neat column of shillings and cents posted on the school board by Mr Heavens.

That day I finished at about five with a tin so full that it swung lazily with the weight of wealth. I was cycling home triumphantly, and as I always did, rounded the corner at the junction between Salim and Makupa Roads oblivious to the sedate blink of the traffic lights.

About five yards ahead, two policemen barred the road and shouted out in Swahili.

'Hey Indian, where are you going? Can't you see the red light?'

Within an hour I was in jail.

I was taken to the police station adjoining Naaz cinema and pushed through a metal grille door into a stonewalled cell. In the hours that followed, the men amused themselves, languidly deriving pleasure from my fear and distress.

'How is the floor, Boy? Your mother coming? We're looking forward to having her here.'

It was a good introduction to the language of uniformed power, ethnic humour and racial hatred. In time, I would hear countless dialects of this tongue spoken fluently across the world.

I waited hungrily, sitting on the damp floor of the cell, wondering what makes a Kenyan a Kenyan. I knew the answer the policemen would have given. I saw a prophecy in their eyes. My parentage and colour had become a curse. I thought of India, and Bibiji then; ancient roots and migratory routes that had remorselessly brought me to this point.

It was hours before my father appeared, mysteriously, after midnight. I was too relieved to ask how he had found me there. He looked troubled, and typically for him at that time of night, he had lost his usual sense of humour. He paid a spot fine to secure my release, and barely spoke as we made our way home. It was a shade of silence I had not experienced before and brought back the tide of fear I thought I had left behind in the jail.

A few days later as I was leaving the morning school assembly, the headmaster, Mr Woods, summoned me to his study. My sojourn in prison had not been an 'event' in the school; there had been no ribbing, no addition to the plethora of jokes that grew out of the playground, not even a mention by the class teacher or the thespian, Mr Heavens. I knew that everybody knew what had befallen me, and yet there had been only a flat hush.

Mr Woods leaned against his desk. He was a sprightly, handsome man with a flashing smile. Standing in his office, with a hundred private sins in my mind, I faced him with dread.

'I'm sorry for what happened last Saturday,' he said. 'I have tried to get an apology from the police commissioner for your parents, but have failed. Please tell them I am sorry for what happened. Unfortunately, I received no help from the Education Department either... These are strange times. The climate is changing in a way I can't live with. I will be leaving the school at the end of this term.'

Our school sat on the edge of a cliff. He looked out from his window at the sea below and let the sea breeze run through his brown hair. 'But I'll miss this place,' he added.

Then he turned to me. 'And you, young man, I brought you to this school, picked you out from a pile of applicants. You haven't disappointed. Tell your parents that they should consider leaving this country. It isn't ready for independent minds, and you are a natural rebel. I've always liked that about you.'

I took his words to heart, but I didn't pass on his advice to my parents.

The wind changed direction in the months and years that followed. It now came from the interior – stronger, darker, more urgent and pungent, with different and inviolable demands. It brought clouds that rained Jomo Kenyatta's picture everywhere. Every school, shop, office and newspaper carried the salt-and-pepper-bearded photograph of the president, or 'Mzee' – 'The Old Man', as he was generally called. The Indians said it as reverently as everyone else, but the sound was deeper, elongated: 'Mm-zaa-hay', as if the extremity of the word was stuck in the throat with a touch of fear and needed greater effort to be expunged.

Traffic stopped immediately when He came to Mombasa. Cyclists dismounted, buses paused in the middle of the road, and street vendors hurriedly handed over a roasted cassava and closed off all deals as the president's motorcade approached. Sometimes the long convoy of Mercedes Benzes would go slowly, and we would stretch out to receive a benedictory wave from Kenyatta's iconic giraffe-tail whisk. A mixture of excitement, relief and exhaustion would run through the crowd.

One morning, just as I cycled up to the school entrance, the president's first batch of motorcycle outriders came screeching by with their left hands waving. We jumped our bikes onto the pavement, joining the other students standing on the kerbside in our all-white school uniforms. To our right, with its nose barely intruding into the main road and the rest of its body in the school driveway, was a cream-coloured Peugeot with a black African driver. A row of cars, also seeking to leave the school grounds, began stacking up behind the Peugeot. Blocked there, unable to go forward or back, the driver sat still. The scene was set: we waited for the cavalcade to come round the bend. No one had ever seen a presidential jink at speed.

The Mercs came faster than sound, like wind and lightning before the clap of tropical thunder. We peered intently to look through the plates of smoked glass that wailed by, sheltering the president from the morning light, and from us. The final car in the convoy braked to a halt in front of the grille of the Peugeot. Four men in dark suits emerged. One opened the door, another pulled the driver from behind the wheel, and then all four pummelled his body into a bloody heap.

| *Harambee, Harambee:* | Let's pull together, let's pull together |
| *Tu imbe pamoja:* | Let's sing together |

Harambee, Harambee: Let's pull together, let's pull together
Tu jenga Kenya yetu: Let's build our Kenya together

Sometimes people hummed Kenyatta's anthem as we waited for the motorcade to pass. It was a prosaic, addictive ditty, which you could not afford not to know. It spanned the spaces between the races – a swaying, uneven footbridge across a chasm. We had learnt to sing it on the fringes of public rallies. The Indians would mime meekly, politely following the exultant cadences of black Africans, as both groups tasted body smells they had never before encountered at close quarters. The rallies were held on the same open fields where, years ago, we had waited with irrepressible excitement for the night to come, and for the Omo van with the bright white screen to transport us to Tarzan's Africa.

Sometimes the mood would change suddenly. A black politician would take the microphone, and work the crowd into frenzy with a populist refrain.

'Indians must assimilate; they must let us marry their women.'

Later, at the temple, I would observe Gujarati women huddling around my grandmother after the evening *aarti*. They would fidget, tighten and retighten their saris, repeating a sentence that the prayers hadn't succeeded in washing away.

I completed my A-levels at boarding school in December 1971. I was eighteen when I left Lenana Secondary School, then one of the top schools in the country and, once, the haven for Settler scions who still spoke of it as the 'Duke of York High'. I don't recall thinking of Bibiji much during those joyless and violent years cloistered in the Ngong Hills.

The days at the school were contained within evangelical certainties that beget bigotry. We rose to a Christian assembly in shoes that had to be polished absolutely spotless, and finished with character-forming sports – rugger or cross-country runs – and a precise clock-ticking hour of evening prep. Then, a reading from the Bible, a preserve of the prefects, with the narrowed eyes of Mr Humphreys, the house master, scanning the benches for the remotest hint of disrespect, with that same hungry, punitive alertness at 8pm that he brought to the morning drill when he hunted for splayed knots in the striped maroon-and-silver school ties, and dullness in the creases of grey trousers.

In between the sterility of chemistry and physics labs and the vectors of maths, there were the unexpected tangents of the new post-colonial curriculum. This only really touched us in the general studies class, when we would come alive for a frenzied hour. There was a sadistic pleasure to our unequal tussle with the Welsh chaplain whose anachronistic homilies we relished twisting into apoplectic rage. These rhetorical skills were honed in the debating club and over sour, exeat-cancelled weekends when we rehearsed the liberating radicalism of *Transition*, the Pan-Africanist magazine produced by the Ugandan-Indian, Rajat Neogy.

Neogy drew on the virtuosity of provocative minds from across the continent: Wole Soyinka, Chinua Achebe and Chris Okigbo from Nigeria, Cameron Duodo from Ghana, Dennis Brutus and Nadine Gordimer from South Africa, Ali Mazrui from Kenya, and, two non-Africans, VS Naipaul and Paul Theroux. It was a rare and astonishing magazine, which ranged polemically across poetry and politics. It brought an edgy, new thrill to our lives, of being in the company of bigger minds; brilliant, prophetic writers who were critical, brave and unbounded.

But there was also a delusionary myopia and fatal immaturity to our intellectual verve. We chose not to see Neogy's incarceration by the Uganda government for sedition, the lights going out around him at Makerere University, the brief stay of the magazine when it relocated to Accra and its inevitable death by political asphyxiation, starved of the same air that we could feel becoming thinner around us. We dismissed the prescient clarity of Naipaul, and the studied irreverence of Theroux, who we saw as outsiders entering our African conversation.

Ironically, it was the writing of these two, and a brilliantly incisive and empathetic Polish travel-writer, Ryszard Kapuscinksi, whose work I would come across much later, that would provide resonance, comfort and meaning to my peripatetic life in the decades to come.

Ultimately, beneath the bravura of belittling a dead past and a wrinkled missionary who, I would learn many years later, would die on the ship 'home' and be buried at sea, we were just children of the age. We learnt to fabricate expedient commonalities and slap the label of 'other' and 'outsider' on someone else. Then at night, in the darkness, we turned on each other, possessed by the endemic culture of physical and spiritual violence starkly magnified by that British public school. Our individual identities disappeared and our ethnicity shone in the gloom, inviting attention and abuse. As Kamau, the house bully, wandered drunk through the dorms with a knife in his hand, Okwach was no longer 'Joe'; he lost his forename and became 'the Luo', while I, the usual favoured prey, became 'that Indian'.

It was a good time for silence. I would lie still in bed, unable to define myself and listen as a paedophilic housemaster – 'Pog the homo', we called him – came to collect a junior from the bed at the end of the dorm. He was as soundless as an elephant in the dark. He would ease his large frame and jutting potbelly sideways through the door. The boy would rise, find his glasses and slip into shoes without a sound and follow closely, white and black ghosting into the night in a blink.

Kenya and Uganda had no Nyerere, Mandela or Tutu to mould a transcendental language that would have enabled us to make peace with each other and explore the richness of our multiple identities. We had Kenyatta and Uganda had Obote, corrupt murderous tyrants in the making, and mere pacesetters at that. At eighteen, I could see the divisions racing towards me. The East Africa into which I had been born had splintered to become Tanganyika, Uganda and Kenya. But the fissures had not stopped there. They spread wider and deeper – chaotic, crackling fractals of race, tribe and language, fragmenting every pane of Kenyan society and entering that dormitory with brutal inevitability.

I went to sleep on the shards of a shattered and contested identity, in the regulation pyjamas we were compelled to wear to cover cheap, shapeless vests; a single, tiny black earpiece in my left ear; my hands under the blue blankets twiddling the dials of a prized Sanyo radio, switching in vain between the stiff, humourless channels on the Voice of Kenya.

When I returned home to Mombasa from boarding school at the end of 1971, I found the future had arrived before me.

My father had lost his job as the Africanisation process gathered pace. He had been a manager of a small English-owned hardware agency and had been replaced by Benjamin, a young African protégé. Father roller-coasted through a few days of dejection, but soon recovered his cheer. If anything, he seemed revived by the certainty of his bleak future in Kenya.

'It's their country; it's their right. Africa is for Africans. And anyway, that's our fate; there is no security for Indians anywhere in the world.'

He said that often and always with a laugh that calibrated the space between us; he was an Indian-Indian, while I had only ever known the pulse of Africa. Years later, I saw that he had been laughing at himself and the Indian immigrants and White settlers who were lost in an illusion of permanence on a continent where the firmament was changing, the stars realigning to signal the way out for lighter-skinned interlopers.

That December, as 1972 approached, it became clear that my parents were committed to emigrating. I cycled around Mombasa – the explorations of an imminent exile, sketching maps for memory. The godowns around Kilindini Harbour were filled with the silenced orchestras of fleeing Indian households: mortars and pestles, tiffins and steel tumblers, altar bells and *puja* conch shells, refereeing whistles and melodious harmoniums.

Families who knew little of what Canada or Britain beheld packed possessions for every conceivable emergency: children's spinning tops and frayed leather volleyballs, tinny torches and spare light bulbs, shirt buttons and jute-needles, bottles of mustard oil, sherbet and rose syrup. Years later, I would see the moulding detritus in Formica cabinets in Birmingham, London and Manchester.

I peddled to my previous schools and sports clubs, past shops where I had drunk bottles of Coke on tick. Mr Woods had been right; the climate had changed and so had the ecology – new evangelical churches and freshly painted road signs, football being played on open fields latticed by meandering tracks scuffed by the bare feet of rural migrants, vacant residential plots tilled with maize and cassava. I cycled up Changamwe Hill to the drive-in cinema, the largest temple in town to the gods of Hindi films. Its metal gates were padlocked, the towering screen a film of grey-green mildew.

Teachers and tailors, chemists and cobblers, train drivers and bookkeepers had gone or there was news that they were leaving. Indian cricket and hockey clubs were putting aside rivalries going back generations to keep the sports alive by combining and playing scratch seven-a-side games.

Only one ritual seemed to have survived and that too had an air of impending demise: the littoral walk that Indian families took in droves every day at dusk on Mama Ngina Drive. There were fewer Indian families, and most simply sat in their cars out of fear of the increasing numbers of black Africans now sharing the promenade. My father typically laughed this paranoia away and set off briskly towards the lighthouse, as was his evening wont. We fell into step, our breath resonating. I had always endeavoured to match his stride, taking heart in the approaching parity as I grew in height. It was perhaps the sweetest of all the activities I shared with him while he was alive.

That evening my head was filled with a stew of late-teen hormones, multiple, rootless identities and an abstract future.

'I want to go to India,' I said.

'To India? What for? To eat dung?' he replied.

'It's where we're from. I want to see where we are from. I want to go to our village.'

He laughed as I smarted. 'It's where we have run away from. You're lucky you weren't born there. Otherwise you'd be eating cow shit now.'

I felt happy; he hadn't said 'no'. He had said nothing new and had not slackened his brisk pace. We reached the lighthouse and turned back, walking silently, apace, in the darkness together, the waves crashing onto the coral outcrops below us. I suspect he too loved this shared walk, the only activity he now did with me, his eldest son, since the distant days of the multiplication tables and tests of division.

Two months later, we went together to the port to collect my ticket to Bombay on the steam ship, Karanja. An alien coalition of metal, formality and geometric shapes now ruled over the Kilindini Docks. Where I had once swivelled my bicycle to turn south to explore the crags overlooking the mangroves of Mtongwe, there was now tarmac, marked out with white lines. Black African officers in immaculate white uniforms bestrode the harbour. Grey warehouses, yellow cranes and stacks of multi-coloured cubic containers stood where once there had been trees whose secrets I knew – a tart mango here, a sweet cashew apple there.

At the back of the port estate, far from the deep-sea berths, was a bland single-storey block with a low ceiling. Two pallid Indian clerks were dealing with a gaggle of Indian customers.

'Here you are Maash-ter,' father said, as he handed me the tickets that were to take me 'home' to a village in a land I had never seen. The usual twinkle in his eyes played hide-and-seek among shadows thrown up by his own buried memories. I had planned to talk to him that day about Bibiji, but too many other emotions were coursing between us. My mind had also latched onto the word he had used to address me. I glowed when he called me 'Master'. It was when he was being affectionate. Or when he thought I was being too full of myself.

We fell into step instead, walking back to the car. We never did create a language to talk about his past, about Bibiji.

Chapter Two

THAT FIRST VISIT to India in February 1972, began with the customs man.

Spindly, bow-legged coolies invaded the *SS Karanja* as soon as the gangway was put in place. They led the procession down the plank carrying metal trunks and hay-roll bundles of bedding on their turbaned heads, their hungry eyes bulging with strain. They brought us to earth with their guttural commands and untrustworthy haste. Gingerly, I found the uneven treads on the walkway. All the passengers were holding tightly onto their lifebelts for land: sling bags and bundles of money, jewellery, passports and papers.

We entered a dark shed with rows of long, low benches. On these, trunks and bundles had been set out before a handful of customs officers in tired uniforms. I found a space and laid down my offering: a canvas rucksack and green sleeping bag. One of the customs men walked slowly towards my belongings. It was when he spoke that I recognised him. It was Pran, the ubiquitous alcohol swilling, womanising nemesis of every hero in every Hindi movie I had ever seen. The cigar was missing, but the wisps of smoke rose in my imagination.

'What's in here?'

He had that predatory look of boredom, alertness and pitilessness that has been perfected by customs officers around the world through generations of public service. I mumbled a string of nothings. His nostrils, as they did on screen, flared momentarily. He rocked his head slowly, sipping the fear in my answer.

'What have you for me?' His eyebrows and forehead rose with the question.

I gawked at him, immobilised by the clarity with which I could hear him in the cacophony that filled the shed. I had hidden £200 in travellers' cheques against my right groin in a pocket stitched inside the front of my trousers by an Indian tailor in Mombasa, wise to the embraces of Indian pickpockets. In my normal left-hand side pocket was a bundle of Indian rupee notes stained with history. They had come a long way.

My father had left his village in Punjab at the age of 19 in 1949, with two rupees and a BSc graduation certificate to lose along the way. He had been lent the money by a relative for a day's ride by *tonga*, a horse and cart, from the nearby town of Hoshiarpur to the distant hamlet of Doraha, 'the place where two roads pass', in Ludhiana district where Bibiji was born. There he had borrowed again and boarded a train that ran on the late 19th century line built by the British from Peshawar in the North West Frontier, through Lahore, Amritsar, and on to Delhi. He barely paused in Delhi. It was flooded with Punjabis like himself, but most were refugees from what had now become Pakistan after the bloodletting that accompanied the partition of British India two years earlier. They had not survived a genocidal rite of passage to give away their gains to more recent internal migrants of independent India. He moved on.

He reached Bombay, the *filmi* city of silvery dreams, and found his first job selling Remington typewriter ribbons door-to-door. At night, he slept on the same desk from which he began his working day. It was a worthy trailer for a life's vocation as an unyielding salesman. Meanwhile, across the sea, his sister, Savitri Bua, was peddling an inch-square photograph of him among families with marriageable daughters. In June 1952, he secured the best deal of his short life, escaping from India with the winning hand of the 'girl from Africa' – my mother.

In the twenty years since my father had migrated to Kenya, Indian nationalism had painted populist new vistas to excite patriotism at home and homesickness in the diaspora. The Nehru dynasty, first Jawarlal and then Indira, had declared socialist crusades against poverty, and fought three bankrupting wars with the country's immediate neighbours. Five quinquennial development plans had produced, in Nehru's words, 'new temples of the new India', dams and factories. If nothing else, these had generated droning, self-congratulatory commentaries after the evening news on All India Radio in flawless, highbrow English by presenters with cultivated accents.

And there was the export of Indian religiosity. An outlandish mix of charismatic mystics, tantrics, Vedantists and yogis – among others, Bhagwan Shree Rajneesh, Maharishi Mahesh Yogi, Bhaktivedanta Swami Prabhupada, Paramhansa Yogananda, Swami Sivananda – had transformed Hinduism's tawdry image into a fashionable spirituality, drawing Rolls-Royced American and British rock stars, Western European intellectuals and a generation of already-high hippies to look up to India. Even the Iron Curtain had opened silkily for India. Dramatic translations of the great Hindu epics, *The Ramayana* and *The Mahabharata*, had appeared across the USSR and its satellite states – not just in Russian, but also in Hungarian and Polish. The story went that it was not the draught of the Cold War, but these spiritual currents that brought the Soviet Premier, Nikita Khrushchev, to India twice in four years, and transformed a hardened communist into a theologian. When asked of his impressions of India,

Khrushchev is said to have responded, 'The only proof I know of the existence of God is that India works'. And India didn't just work; it did so with song and dance. The worlds' largest democracy had felt confident enough to divorce the world's oldest democracy, and grow its offspring alone, nurturing Bollywood into the biggest global film and fantasy industry.

But none of this had been enough to bring my father back to India. It hadn't even cleansed his memory of the universality of cow dung. So here I was, retracing his journey, on the wings of his fortune.

Prowling Pran, the customs man, leaned towards me, sniffing for a share of this wealth.

'*Khaaayyy?*' He repeated the 'what' in Hindi and suffixed it with a malignant 'hhuuuhh', as he did on screen. 'Have you got something for me?'

I fingered the currency in my pocket. I had taken less than a hundred steps on Indian soil. Ahead lay a thousand-mile journey to the ancestral home in Northern Punjab, yet I couldn't see past the transparent wickedness standing before me. I handed over a sliver of notes – 200 rupees, maybe more. He pocketed them as he put a chalk mark on my bags and dismissed me with an upward and diagonal nod towards the exit.

My cousin, Savitri Bua's eldest daughter, was waiting outside. She took charge immediately, as a host invariably does in a rapacious city, drawing on her memory as an emigrant from Kenya. We took a ferry to her house, which was nestled in a creek on the mainland ringed by mangroves. For two days, I explored the lush natural surrounds of her house, and played with her two-year-old daughter, every so often looking across the sea.

Birth, death and reincarnation: the circle that links these three is perhaps the only theological constant in the medley of contrary beliefs that is Hinduism. But even on that matter there is less certainty than there is in the view that Bombay is where all Indians – Hindus, Muslims, Buddhists, Christians, Sikhs, Parsees and Atheists – go to be reborn as stars.

I died there in February 1972.

I had arrived in Bombay with a distinct, if twisted and incomplete sense of selfhood, anchored in being visibly different. Indians in Africa were a minority, a race apart. That was a plain fact. It had been legally so under the colonial administration, and while political independence had removed the 'colour bar', it had also meant that Indians were even more visibly a minority. As emigrating Indians fled from Uhuru – 'freedom' – their houses, jobs and schools were seamlessly filled by black African neighbours. Language, that fluid and living instrument of consciousness, failed to heal the rupturing fabric. It did not lead us through these changes. We remained Indians. There was no place yet for African-Indians, or Indian-Africans.

On the morning of my third day in India I crossed the thin channel from the mainland to Bombay proper. At about eleven in the morning I found the building I had come in search of. I walked onto the second-floor balcony across the road from the Victoria Railway Station, and drowned there.

Below me were a million people who all looked exactly like me, surging and ebbing with that irregular relentlessness of a sea-tide. I felt my 'self' dissolving into nothingness, stripped of distinctiveness, utterly irrelevant. It was as if I had entered into a universe of a million mirrors and forgotten which body I belonged to. My 'self' dissipated and floated away. I lost consciousness of my ego and body. I have no recollection of how long 'I' was dead.

I was brought back to life by a great-great-uncle of my mother's, Mr Khosla. He held my hand and was dressed, appropriately, in pure white *kurta*-pyjamas, the colour of death and birth. I had come looking for him with greetings from my mother. His narrow balcony overlooked the human tide that lapped Bombay's main railway station.

He took me back into a room in which a dozen or so women sat cross-legged with their backs against the four walls, folding fine strands of saffron into one- and two-inch paper sachets. In the middle of the room was an altar, a shallow heap of the precious stamens from the then halcyon valleys of Kashmir. He introduced me to members of his family who came into the room. They greeted me politely and perfunctorily, doors opening and shutting firmly on a potential leech.

Mr Khosla returned to his white pillows, which rested against the wall that faced the entrance to the room, the patriarch's throne. He sat me by his side and spoke to a woman at the door.

'Bring the food.'

Her startled expression showed that it wasn't time, but she hurried away and returned with his tiffin. He unpacked the trays and placed them before us. A light smile played on his lined face as he asked after my mother and father. He slipped me a couple of rotis and pointed to the vegetables and dhal.

'Eat, Son.'

We took turns at dipping into the tins, while others in the room stole occasional glances. I had last eaten like that as a nine-year-old with my maternal grandfather, Mr Khosla's second cousin. They would have known each other as teenagers in 1919, when the massacre on the park lawns of Jallianwala Bagh in Amritsar irrevocably turned the Punjabis against the British. It was the moment when my land-owning ancestors, from both sides of the family, were forced off the political fence, losing forever the agrarian foundations of their wealth. Mr

Khosla's father had probably begun buying and selling saffron then, mutating their clan name to Khosla, from *Kesar-Wallahs*, the Saffron People.

We finished the meal with a drink of water drawn from a clay pot and poured into steel tumblers. The taste of earthy and metallic minerals stained my tongue like delicate traces of saffron on rice.

Mr Khosla studied me.

'You look like your father, but not as light in complexion. He was even skinnier when I first saw him.' We were on familiar ground. The grading of colour, the straining of history; he was placing me precisely, prejudicially in his memories, using a lexicon developed over centuries.

'I was there when your parents were married at our house in Ville Parle in 1952.'

I grappled with the awkwardness of an intimate thought. My parents here in Bombay twenty years ago, utterly innocent to each other, never having met and smelt each other before; my father about my age, marrying an even shier girl, two years younger than he was. The recollection made him laugh aloud.

'Good woman, your mother. She arrived from Africa on Saturday with her mother – just the two of them, mother and daughter. We held the marriage ceremony in our courtyard the very next day. Your father and mother sailed to Africa a few days later.'

He repeated the praise for my mother twice, each time with a pregnant silence that suggested unspeakable stories. I said goodbye soon after we had finished eating, innocent to the finality of our parting. I think he knew that he would never see me again. He had made sure we shared an early lunch, honouring the gossamer of a shared and diverging ancestry.

I made no attempt, then or soon after, to decipher the cryptic silences he had placed loudly before me. Decades later, I discovered why he had pointed to my mother. She had suffered quietly in his presence on her wedding day, and he had followed the story of her married life from afar. That day at the Khosla's house, my maternal grandmother had presented a dowry of jewellery and cash to Bapu, my paternal grandfather. True to his gambler's nature, Bapu had upped the stakes and asked for more.

My mother had sat weeping by the nuptial fire. Beside her, also veiled, his face still unseen by her, and wearing a wide-brimmed leather hat, sat my father. Somewhere in the background of that fading picture I had looked at often as a child, Bapu had been counting the money he had successfully extracted. He sent some of the cash to Amritsar to pay the admission fees to medical school for one of his other sons, my father's younger brother. My mother remembers him scrupulously weighing the gold in the dowry the day after the wedding to make sure that every final grain of promise had been received.

Throughout his own marriage, Bapu had failed to bring in sufficient money to feed the family and honour Bibiji's consuming dream that her children be educated. He had dealt with his own inadequacy by selling off Bibiji's jewellery. Bibiji had sustained the family and fed her brood by eking out an income giving tuition to the children of wealthier landowners, which saved the family from destitution at the cost of her ever-weakening body. After she died, he used the marriage of his sons to extract punitive dowries, pointing to the merits of his sons – qualities that Bibiji had instilled – to up their value. It had made my father hate the dowry system with greater passion than he brought to his marriage.

Bibiji's shadow had crossed my parents' marriage in the Khosla house. Bapu had invoked her dreams without any shame or sense of irony around the fact that he was depriving my parents of a chance to begin their own family with resources in hand. All this I was to discover in time. I left Mr Khosla oblivious to the economic transactions that had underpinned my arrival in this world, ignorant of the calculations that lay behind the romanticised institution of arranged marriages. Years later, when I asked my mother about that day and the years that followed, and if she ever fell in love with my father, she replied simply: 'There was no love in those days.'

Then, after a pause, she had added, 'Marriages are preordained. When things are meant to be, they just are.'

It was not like her to parrot received beliefs. I knew she had thought over her life deeply, and that there must have been myriad synchronicities of certainty before she would have accepted the humbling authority of this aphorism.

'We were married on Saturday, 28 June 1952. The Monday after our marriage, your father and I left the Khosla's house to take a train to the Passport Office. It was raining torrentially that day. Bombay monsoons. As the train left the station we saw a man running along the platform, scrambling to board. Your father stretched his hand out and pulled him onto the train.

'Your father had no passport, and the waiting time for documents was months and that too with bribes along the way. We got your father's documents in three days, and sailed to Mombasa the following Saturday.

'The man your father had helped onto the train worked at the Passport Office'.

As I left the premises of the *Kesar-Wallahs* I joined a dense crowd moving away from the railway station. I looked around. Near here, two ancient family lines had intersected. I had met an old man who had granted space in his own house for my story to begin. I would now carry the account to another generation as my story.

I felt exhilarated. Just two hours before, I had felt my 'self' die. Now, I was walking through a crowd of thin, sweaty Indian men and women heavy with a spicy, putrid odour at the end of the working day. Around me Bombay teemed restlessly, garish and squalid. A towering poster of Dev Anand's latest movie, *Hare Rama, Hare Krishna*, stretched across the roof of a building ahead. Its brazen irreverence incited playfulness: 'A must-see, *masti* (mischief) hit...'

I smiled, taking pleasure in the *khitchri* of a small, fractured mind that had produced a weak pun. Somehow it felt in tune with the melange of India and the sauciness with which Bombay had turned a sacred mantra into the title of a cult movie and an eponymous pop song. Around the corner Indira Gandhi's edict was splattered on a long cream wall: '*Garibi Hatao*' – Abolish Poverty. Brown stains of urine and rotting mounds of rubbish had been deposited under the red lettering. I was alive to the perverse obedience and chronic irony abundant in India.

A few days later I met up with another cousin. She was an artist who had recently returned from Europe and had found work with a prominent national fashion house. She was battling to reconcile commercial imperatives with fine art, and adjust to India after years living in England and Finland. With her was an American friend. Struggling to make sense of India, I poured out a stream of anecdotes. I spoke of being stripped of the bedazzling images that had filled the Panavision screens of Naaz, Regal, Queen's and Moon's, the cinemas of my childhood in Mombasa. Where was the Arcadian motherland that had shimmered to the melodies of OP Nayyar's music?

Travelling cheap, and mostly around urban settlements, I had seen crude concrete buildings and burgeoning slums along the rutted roads; families sleeping on the pavements; the black gunk of oil, excrement and decaying waste by the food stalls of street vendors;

armies of skinny dark brown women in ragged saris, their children in tow, collecting shit; flies, foul smells and persistent beggars whenever I sat to eat; holy cows grazing on piles of rubbish and brushing past me with the disdain of a corrupt priest; the ceaseless din of traffic horns and the crush of people; clouds of black flies settled like raisins on trays of sweet *jalebis*.

On an overnight train, I had seen the sun rise on rows of dark bums adjacent to the railway line, defecating as the train clunked past, each body shamelessly assured of personal hygiene with a clay or brass beaker of toilet water beside it. Meanwhile, I had become unnaturally preoccupied with my insides, my stomach churning from diarrhoea to wilful constipation within a single day.

My cousin laughed.

'Come on, didn't you read Naipaul before you set out?'

I was embarrassed. I hadn't known that VS Naipaul's sojourn at Makerere had been preceded by a journey to India.

'VS Naipaul. *India: An Area of Darkness*', said the blonde American.

They were insistent that I should read the book before going further. I felt irked, challenged and a touch insulted that I should need a guidebook or a grand theory, and that too by a travel writer I had pooh-poohed. Unfamiliar with this genre, I had gravitated instead to a simplistic view derived from poorly taught history classes in early secondary school that travel was essentially a Livingstonian journey of wide-eyed, visual discovery.

As I listened to my cousin and her friend, I had my first vicarious taste of the power of travel books. Naipaul offered them a lens to understand the decay of India. His piercing analysis, despite an inherent despair and cynicism, was for them a rationalising filter that helped them cope. Obstinately, I closed my eyes to Naipaul's *Darkness*, content – if travelling in India could ever evoke that word

– to commit my energies to surviving another day and suffering for myself the wretchedness that Naipaul prophesied.

Nonetheless, there were times when I wished I had help; a way of seeing and being that could help me make sense of the huge, frenetic and exhausting canvas in which I was now immersed. Wistfully, I would recall the naivety with which I had visualised this trip: as a search for Bibiji and an understanding of my ancestry. This desire for renewed purpose and existential meaning would come as readily on a vendor's bench sipping chai as it would on a slow train filled with the smells, artefacts and Hessian sacks of peasants.

Amidst this raw collage that swamped my senses were stills of mystery that offered glimpses of another country. In Mora, on the mainland, a ferry ride across from Bombay, I had gone in search of a rustic temple reputedly hidden in a grove. I found instead a young woman returning from a well. Her hips swayed as she danced away with a conic tier of three water pots erect and still on her head, each voluptuous copper body snug on the one below. Her long shining black plaits fell back to caress a slim waist. In that fleeting moment, as she turned her face and our eyes met, I saw her spirit leap. It burnt an enduring question on my mind. Did she fly or die when Bombay sprawled over and ate that patch of green?

That was a rare moment. In those first three weeks, my energy mostly went on retaining my foothold and protecting my resources in a landscape that was larger, noisier, busier and more fervid than anything I had experienced before in Kenya. Caste and karma; class and colonialism; a new democracy with new dynasties; sexual prudence and an exploding population; Partition and ever-present Pakistan; interminable stories of Hindus and Muslims, entwined by blood, history, hate, and boundless, invisible daily kindnesses; books, books, books on every pavement, and endemic illiteracy staring one in the face; symbols of faith and spirituality on bodies, trees and rickshaws, and dehumanising poverty at every step. India's angles were simply too varied, complex and askew for my mind.

But gradually I coped better, and every few days I would retreat into my diary, my words usually falling into a tone that was sorrowful, petty, unsophisticated, enfeebled by the sensory assaults of the claustrophobic vistas through which I was moving. These private attempts to make sense of my journey invariably revolved around the same questions. They came not from the large Nehruvian frame of 'what is India?' Or Naipaul's probing 'why is India like this?' But rather infinitesimally, 'Am I really Indian? How Indian am I?'

It was from that pathetic base of individuality, out of a preoccupation with ego, that I constructed personal dramas of self-affirmation. I usually did this when provoked by a prosaic injustice, like the incident in the customs hall in Bombay. That particular experience – Pran's extortion of a bribe – followed me, regularly changing guise. It caught up with me once more in Baroda while I was queuing for a rail ticket out of the city.

'If you want a ticket, I'll get you one. But it will cost. You won't get a ticket without paying something extra.' The offer came from a teenager, no older than me.

'But I'm a foreigner. I was told I could. I have my passport on me.'

On this occasion, with time on my hands and a good night's sleep behind me, I declined. A while later, I had a fair price ticket. The boy was waiting for me in his ill-fitting faded-purple nylon shirt, flapping loose grey trousers and blue-strapped plastic sandals. He greeted me quizzically. I showed him my prize. We laughed. I swaggered onto the train in an even better mood, but not without a flash of karmic anxiety that bad luck was bound to follow such good fortune.

I considered India more benevolently when I was happier. As the train cut its way through Gujarat's countryside, I feasted on the unfailingly cheerful saris of the peasant women: bright reds and brilliant yellows exuberant in a parched land thirsting for the monsoons. I saw families of pilgrims carrying bedrolls, food and infants, chanting *kirtans* as they marched briskly on. They could have been walking three hundred miles to the sea, to one of the four holiest sites of Hinduism, Lord Krishna's capital of Dwarka, or they could have been on their way to the shrine of a local Muslim Sufi saint with supernatural powers. They wore their fervour with the same ease and constancy as their timeworn peasant clothes.

It was the film scene I had been waiting for: rustic, romantic, set to the beat of a slowly moving train and blessed with a big blue sky and bucolic lines. Bizarrely, it made me think of Pran, everyone's favourite film villain and part-time customs man.

I decided then, that 'customs' men – and they were all men in that era before the needle of feminism lanced that boil in the civil service in the 1980s and 1990s – were aptly named. They wake you up to the mores of a people. Untroubled by any familiarity with Naipaul's writing, I decided that he would not have arrived at this insight. It was a pleasurable reverie, and made me feel clever and sanguine about encounters to come.

And so it proved, not just for the remainder of my time in India but well beyond; for decades of passage through the portals of the alphabet across continents.

In the 1970s, travelling by coach across Europe, I crossed the border from France to Holland on my way to Amsterdam. All the passengers were asked to alight. I stood by my rucksack. A few hours earlier, we had undergone a similar ritual when entering France. There, the French had been unashamedly enthusiastic in their scrutiny of Arab, Asian and black African passengers. Now a tall, broad Dutch officer stood before us, not much older than me. He would have been in his mid-twenties. My head of Jimi Hendrix hair and gold-rimmed, round John Lennon glasses were met with a half-smile.

'Student? Amsterdam?' It was a laconic, unfussy exchange with the directness and economy of a brisk people ready to run and stick a finger in a dyke. He swung his left thumb towards the bus. 'Enjoy your time there.'

A few years later, I was in Blantyre. I arrived by air via Johannesburg on a plane carrying a handful of Malawian officials and South African businessmen. They were all swept through the airport by waiting minders. Malawi was then an apartheid-friendly country, ruled by Hastings Banda, a Presbyterian medical doctor. Dr Banda had appointed himself President-for-Life and fused Self, Party and State. Independence had come to mean a drab, stable state where a megalomaniac leader ruled by fiat, dispensing favours and fear whimsically.

I was stopped at customs by an officer who asked me to open my suitcase. It was the only piece of luggage on a long metal rack in a cavernous modern hall. It held little. I was travelling light and had even shorn my curls before setting off for Malawi, having heard of mandatory haircuts at overland border crossings.

There was no African warmth – just the cold stare of a customs officer who had found nothing of consequence. I attempted to lighten the encounter and pointed to the handful of rhumba, Afro-jazz and township music cassettes with my Walkman. 'Good music...'

It was a cue that could have easily led to a ready laugh and warm banter, as it had done in neighbouring Zambia. Instead, I saw a momentary flicker in his eyes as he studied the tapes, and then a spiritless, vacant detachment. I was to encounter this sour deadness often in Banda's Malawi. A nation that gave its name to an extraordinary lake – long, deep and moody, with the greatest biodiversity of fish in any freshwater lake on Earth – had been turned into a climate-controlled trout farm. And a trout stood before me with bulging eyes and an open mouth.

Then, in 1997, an assignment took me to Colombo. I brought with me some of my earliest childhood stories. Lanka was the island kingdom of the ten-headed King Ravana. It was here that Ravana held Queen Sita prisoner after capturing her with a shape-shifting ploy of deceit. Growing up, I had sat through countless recitals of *The Ramayana* enthralled by this unsettling tale of Good and Evil, where right and wrong never seemed straightforward. There was one episode in this epic which had remained fast and apart from the moral cubism of the story: the audacity of the monkey-king, Hanuman, to rescue Sita by building a bridge of stones across the sea from India to Lanka for his army of animals. It was a gripping, vibrant image of arrival: trumpeting elephants and shrieking apes, leading Rama's troops across a frothing sea to reclaim a beautiful Queen. Hanuman's ingenuity was suffused in my mind with the soaring melodic lilt of my maternal grandmother's recitations.

The plane landed just after noon. There was only one other plane on the expansive concrete apron, which was edged with young soldiers in army fatigues bunkered behind sand bags. Anti-aircraft cannons pointed at a clear blue sky. The country was at war again, but the scene before me was lifeless and sparse, a world bleached of colour and sound leaving behind fear and silence.

I had read many conflicting narratives to explain this war. There was one thread that ran through all of them: a government of Sinhalese Buddhists fighting Tamil-Hindu rebels. The labels were as unavoidable as they were incoherent. They made no theological sense given the centrality of religious tolerance in both faiths, and the fact that the Tamil Tigers had in fact been formed and were led by a nihilistic Tamil-Christian, Velupillai Prabhakaran.

I handed my passport to the Customs Officer. He stared long at it, as had happened moments earlier at the immigration counter. My suitcase stood unopened. He was more concerned with what was within me: my roots and loyalties, the prejudices I was carrying and the filters in my eyes. He read out my first name, more common in South India as a Hindu surname. He was clearly displeased with the order of names in the identity document, as if in arranging it that way I was trying to slip something vital past him.

'Mr Rajan. You Indian?' Border controls everywhere in the world are promontories of officialdom where the air is thin; there is little oxygen for nuanced identities alloyed from an amalgam of ethnicity, geography and personal choice.

I smiled weakly. 'My parents were Indian...'

He studied my British passport. 'Born in Aaff-Reek-Aa, eh?'

'Kenya,' I replied. That came effortlessly.

He flipped through pages replete with repeat stamps from over a dozen African countries. 'Go.'

I passed through the cracks in his imagination. It would happen often through my life. I would never get used to that liquid feeling.

By the end of February 1972, I had travelled on buses and trains through Maharashtra, Gujarat, Madhya Pradesh and Uttar Pradesh to reach Delhi. The days had become tedium: sourcing a safe hot meal, not being cheated by rickshaw-*wallahs*, savouring cold bottles of Limca pop and hand-squeezed cane juice with a dab of fresh ginger, and, most troublesome, finding a clean toilet where my body could release its waste.

Like most invaders, I paused in Delhi longer than planned. Two of Bibiji's children – one of my father's sisters and one of his brothers – lived there. Neither spoke of the past. Bibiji was dead to their spoken lives. But her ghost floated through their households directing daily routines similar to those of my childhood a continent away: long glasses of milk drained of every last drop, simple vegetarian meals, a blind fixation with arithmetic tables and daily homework, and an absolute belief in the power of the *Gayatri Mantra* to assure the next meal.

These activities were not unique to our extended family; I had seen versions in other homes. But the force with which they were tied together and the script that accompanied their enactment had a primal urgency, which had sometimes entered my father's voice. I heard the same here.

'Eat! Or you will die of hunger.'

'Study! Get educated, you fool, or you'll wander the streets hungry, and die early.'

The purgatory of poverty, and a singular, sure route of escape – a mother's dread – reverberated across generations.

I was drawn into the drama. No resource could be wasted in the households of Bibiji's progeny, and so I was required to help my younger Indian cousins with their mathematics homework. There were two reasons for this: mathematics was seen as a subject fundamental to economic survival, and there was an assumption that its purity as a discipline could not be compromised by the eccentricities of different national curricula.

It added up to an unsettling stay. I had no desire to be a tutor and my cousins wanted exotic distraction, not tutelage. Meanwhile, my uncles and aunts had no interest in talking about the woman whose call had brought me to their houses. I sought escape.

One day I set out to wander aimlessly through the city on the pretext of buying cotton *kurtas* for the warmer days ahead. Winter was nearly over and Baisakhi, the Punjabi spring festival, was approaching. I had already done the main sights of Delhi: watched the great Indian rope trick at the Red Fort from far away enough not to decipher the chicanery, written something trite in the public visitors' book in the grave grounds of the Gandhi Memorial in Raj Ghat, bent over the innumerable varieties of roses in the primly laid gardens of the presidential palace.

I decided to bus around instead. Serendipity gave me a window seat in a city of a million commuters. I fell into a daze despite the sharp-elbowed hustle around me. The city blurred past in a mildewing stream of ugly concrete, overlaid on a thousand-year history: decaying ramparts of forts and *havelis*, moss-covered tombs of Sufi *pirs*, a mosaic of mosques, *gurudwaras* and temples, the green parks that I hadn't yet walked, and the forlorn mausoleums of invincible emperors.

Approaching a roundabout, the bus swerved sharply left before coming to an abrupt halt. To the right, barely ten metres from my window, I saw the splayed feet of man lying on the road. A motorbike was prone, leaking fuel. A young woman in a lightly patterned blue and white sari was standing beside the man's body, strands of her long black hair shaken free. Her eyes were wide open. I could see hundreds of people gathered in a loose arc. No one made an effort to get close to her. It was then that I realised that she was wailing, a sound so primeval that it held back the crowd as she sought to summon a deaf God.

The man's head was crushed flat; tyre treads of blood, flesh and grey running neatly on. A truck stood innocently at the end of the track. For two days and two nights, the images played on and on in my fevered mind. Decades on, they would return to haunt me.

Three days later, I set off north for my ancestral village with the indelible imprint of my first dead body, fresh and red as a spring day in Punjab.

My first stop was Chandigarh, a city designed to be a new state capital. The departing British had given Punjab's historic capital of Lahore to Pakistan. In a fit of pique or delusion, Nehru had turned to the purist French architect, Le Corbusier, to create a metropolis on the plains of Punjab. Among a people where the word for straight – *seedha* – also means a slightly stupid person, the Frenchman had built a city on the straight lines of modern design.

For a week, I explored the wide streets, the perfectly laid out grid of numbered and deliberately nameless residential 'sectors', tombless parks and beggar-free pavements. I found no heart to the city. In that neat perfection of geometric planning, no space had been made for the central bazaars and narrow alleys, which elsewhere braid the thousand castes of India into a race, breathing into each other. The smell of India was faint and elusive though I caught it by the inter-state bus rank and by Punjabi *dhabhas* near the college hostels.

Thousands of East African-Indian immigrants had chosen the city as their final destination; a laager in the unbearably messy country that they had 'returned' to from the sanitised segregation of colonial Africa. I stayed with Savitri Bua and her family. Her histrionics were gone. In Nairobi, she had drawn on the bittersweet passion of nostalgia. Here, there was only the finality of the irrevocable choice. She died of renal failure within months of my meeting her, her kidneys failing in a country resplendent with the smell of urine. She left behind a brood of graduates, including two consultant urologists.

Bapu arrived to meet me at her house in Chandigarh. It was our first encounter since his visit to Mombasa when was I eight years old. Then I had barely reached up to his chest. Now I stood six foot tall in my Bata safari suedes, athletically erect beside his aged stoop. He sized me up, first with a proud and then a reproving look.

'We have to go to Amritsar. You need to know where you come from.'

'But Amritsar isn't where our village is,' I said. 'I want to go to the village; to Bajwara.'

In the next two weeks, I learnt where my obstinate genes had come from. Bapu decided on the choice of buses, *tongas* and rickshaws as we meandered northwest, rather than north. Occasionally, he let me have my way, looking aside when I added a few *paisas* to the miserly fare he always negotiated with rickshaw-*wallahs* so emaciated that their limbs seemed no thicker than the tubes of the bicycle frame.

We stopped in Kapurthala to see my youngest uncle, Bibiji's last child. He had been eight years old when she died. There was an orphan's air of vulnerability about him, spiked with flashes of bitterness and covered with a white-shirted, polyester sheen of flabby comfort worthy of a branch manager of a nationalised bank. These qualities would combine on Bapu's death to produce a will attributed to my grandfather that no other family member would see. It would leave him to claim all the old man's assets, and what remained of our ancestral land.

My uncle received me with affection, immediately setting out to the local sweet shop in the alley below to buy a box of sweets to mark my arrival. Both he and his wife were generous to a fault. And the fault was certainly not theirs. It was just the urban reality of poor lower-middle class Punjab, and it showed how deracinated from my ethnic ancestry I was.

I went up in the world to discover this, to the open roof terrace of my uncle's house. I asked to use the toilet in the morning and was directed up the stairs to a corner of the open terrace. Two bricks were set apart, for squatting feet on a flat slab of concrete. The neighbouring properties, the nearest mere feet away across the narrow alleys of this medieval town, all had identical arrangements.

The deposits of earlier visitors greeted me: mounds of fetid halva. I stood unsure of how to proceed in the public gaze, my discomfort of little interest to the men and young children who came and did their business in a panorama, which would be streaked later in the day by a carnival of kites. Somehow I survived three days, never discovering where and when the women relieved themselves. The only women I saw were the collectors, moving between the houses with buckets on their heads.

Eventually, Bapu relented to my edginess to move on. We headed for Amritsar. He led the way with an imperious ease in his soiled brown *kurta*-pyjamas. We went first to the seat of Sikhism, the Golden Temple. Then, as if responding to a duty to his partisan roots, he suggested we see the neighbouring pallid Hindu imitation, Durgiana Mandir. There was a disinterested restlessness about him as he hurried me through the holy shrines to the real focus of our pilgrimage. It lay five minutes from the outside walls of the Golden Temple.

We walked through a narrow curving passage and emerged into a patch of green. Bapu headed straight towards a low-walled structure to the far right. I was touched by an eerie sensation; the park felt claustrophobic, while the alley spoke of freedom.

'Jallianwala Bagh,' he announced.

The park occupied an area about the size of half a football pitch and was surrounded on all sides by a closely packed stack of two- and three-storey houses. It was hard to reconcile this unkempt common with the idea that it was one of the tipping points of history. British historians estimate that 379 civilians were killed here on 13 April 1919, an oddly precise number for an indiscriminate massacre. Indians estimate the figure as a thousand. What is not disputed is that, after the massacre, Punjabis were made to crawl on their bellies along a street where an English woman had been attacked and, across the state, Indians were required to salute any European they encountered. These actions by the colonial administration had been intended to snip a political bud. Instead, they made the flower bloom into one of the most evocative symbols of the struggle that would end British rule in India and set the sun on the Empire.

Bapu looked me in the eye. He had said nothing when he heard, in Chandigarh, that I had secured a place at a British University.

'I know you are going to study there soon. Don't ever forget what they did to us, what you are and where you have come from.'

Bapu's flourish was cinematic. Family legend had it that he had been one of the survivors of the slaughter, or at least that he had been in Amritsar that day and had helped bring out the bodies piled in the well. He led my fingers to the crumbling mortar on the outside walls of the well where the pockmarks of rifle bullets told their own story. We looked down into the well. 'There were hundreds of bodies in there,' he said.

I didn't ask. It was a good story to go to an English university with.

It took us a day to reach the town of Hoshiarpur. Bajwara was barely two miles away across verdant fields of potatoes and peas. I wanted to hurry on 'home'.

But Bapu was already home. He was now walking with a randomness and gait that I would never know, among shops that held more stories than goods, by ever-lengthening walls that had failed to contain the lusts and betrayals of eternal passions which he too must have fed, past trees that he knew would outlive him by a hundred years, planted by his forebears. I followed him as he collected outstanding dues from his land, caught up with news and converted me into gossip. People called him Lala Soni, a feudal title, a minor lord. He introduced me as his eldest grandson, adroitly making it clear that, of all his sons, my father had been the one who disavowed all interest in his estate. In a society where the covetous chain of inheritance passes immutably through successive generations, my father had stepped freely aside. Bapu's land could never reach me. This fact seemed to quickly extinguish any prospect of future opportunistic interest in me, but lit up distant memories of my father. I wondered later whether that was Bapu's real endowment to me: eliciting the respectful bafflement that my father's name carried.

I looked around with ears that knew this world intimately, but eyes that had never seen it before. At a crossroads in the centre of town stood a clock tower with a black radial dial and cream body, two storeys high. The hands moved unhurriedly over a nondescript face. It was a perfect cipher of the cyclical cosmology of Hinduism: time going round and round carrying life through cycles of creation, dissolution and rebirth. Bibiji would have marked time here. My father had stood here often. I had overheard him reminiscing with a friend about the day they had met here to go together to the friend's neighbouring village of Mandi. It was a conversation between two émigrés recalling narrower school days before the promise of Independent India had faded, impelling them to lives of migration, like wildebeest forever following the scent of the rains. Neither would return here before their death.

We entered Bajwara on a rickshaw. Babar, the first Mogul Emperor, had passed through here in 1525 on his way to conquer Delhi and establish a dynasty that would change forever what it meant to be Indian. My feet touched the source of my ancestry, crunching down upon a patch of sand. It was a familiar sound, of childhood in Mombasa.

I gave the rickshaw-*wallah* a couple of notes – five or ten times the fare. I had the heart not to count. Bapu rebuked me tetchily, but did not ask for the money back from the bewildered man, who was now looking past me at the sight of an approaching riot. A noisy posse of men, women and children were heading our way. An old witch led the group; shrill voiced, wizened, wearing a heavily soiled, ragged sari and waving her arms. She was shouting. 'Rajinder is back! Rajinder is back!'

'Go away Dhantee! What do you want?' said Bapu.

'*Laddoos* – sweets for the whole village,' she replied. 'And *saghan*, a blessing of money, now that your eldest grandson is here.'

She came right up to me and touched my face and hair with her calloused, dark hands, and when she raised them, her knuckles looked like a fan of cinnamon barks. Bapu made a cursory attempt at swearing her away, but it was he who walked off, pleased with the theatre that he had created. He had obviously sent news ahead of our imminent arrival.

'You look just like your father, Rajinder,' she said, as she studied me closely. She had a hoary aura, finely edged by lines of antiquity. She had been the family's toilet cleaner for over two generations and had watched Bibiji die.

Bapu had disappeared. She led me to my father's ancestral house through alleys that were quieter now that the crowd had gone to receive the confectionary that Bapu was distributing. 'A gentle soul; a wonderful man, your father. I knew he would be like that,' she said. 'He was born with the kind eyes of a cow.' It was the ultimate Hindu compliment.

Then, as if she had read the purpose of my quest, she added, 'and a magical singer. The day Bibiji died, he stood on the roof terrace and sang a lament. He sang and he sang until he had brought all the farmers in from the fields.'

Chapter Three

<table>
<tr><td>Kabir kahai:</td><td>Kabir says:</td></tr>
<tr><td>Dus darvazay ka pinjara</td><td>A cage with ten open doors,</td></tr>
<tr><td>Us main panchi paun</td><td>Holds a soul freer than the wind.</td></tr>
<tr><td>Rahai Achamba hoat hai</td><td>The miracle is that it chooses to stay;</td></tr>
<tr><td>Jai Achamba kaun?</td><td>How can you wonder when it goes?</td></tr>
</table>

And then, as the final cadence took flight, my father laughed. We were walking by the Birmingham Reservoir when he recited that poem, reminding me yet again of the wealth of poetry and songs he carried so unassumingly with him, but which I had failed to mine. The words wove themselves into the familiar nasal rhythm of his breath and the squish of our footsteps on the slushy path. I watched the ripples of my father's laughter leave a trace on the water. The lines raced to the other shore where a misshapen dance hall from Britain's age of industrial supremacy stood in disrepair. The echo of that laugh undulated back over the shimmering surface lit by a late English sun and came to rest in my soul.

My father died the following summer, his body fit and lithe with the daily practice of yoga. He was 59. I have the day stark in my mind. I had just reached his sister Swaran Kanta's house in Delhi, having finally returned to India 17 years after that first visit. It was five o'clock in the morning and I had lain down in the spare room to recover from a sleepless night flight from London. I heard the old black phone ring in the corridor, and my aunt shuffling to it from her room next door, muttering words of puzzlement. I opened my eyes to the sound of her scream and the utter clarity of an intuition that my life had changed. I rose unsummoned. She handed me the bone-shaped handset wordlessly. Her big, intelligent eyes were open wide, glazed with tears. My brother was on the line from England. He spoke with unnerving calmness.

'Papaji's gone.'

Those two words carried an absolute finality, the ineffable grief and mystery of bereavement always leading back to that cold fact. Through a numb haze I heard him say that our father had died two hours ago from an aneurysm in the brain. An artery had burst in his head, as he lay asleep. The blood that had spurted out from his ruptured eardrums was still fresh on my parents' pillows in Birmingham as I set out for Delhi's city centre in search of the first available flight back.

I had come to India to renew dormant bonds with my ancestors. I could never have foreseen that the next time I would touch my father his body would be cold in a casket in Wheatley's Funeral Parlour, on an ugly road in the semi-industrial quarter of Balsall Heath.

In the months that followed my father's death, Kabir's poem and my father's accompanying laugh rose often to tease my mind. I would see the verses flying on the wings of Kabir's mysticism, transcending a paradox that I didn't really have the capacity to grasp. One night, visiting my mother, I caught on television Peter Brooke's dramatic production of *The Mahabharata*, created for the Edinburgh Festival. Brooke's interpretation of the epic centred on what he considered one of the most profound questions on the human condition ever asked in literature.

'What is the greatest wonder of them all?' the Gods ask Yudishtra. On the answer rests the lives of Yudishtra's beloved brothers.

'That all around us is the certainty of death, and we live as if we are immortal,' replies Yudishtra.

Weeks before his death, I had glimpsed the equanimity my father had reached with the proximity and inevitability of death. He had come to honour the spirit's choice to accept a sojourn in human life. It made me think about the path my father had taken to arrive at this understanding.

Bibiji's presence lurked in that meditation. I knew that her death had broken his heart, and that out of these fissures had poured songs of anguish that only a night-soil collector had the strength to recall. From that nadir he had moved on to build an inner life that fêted Yudishtra's insight. But, I decided, he hadn't arrived here solely by his own efforts. He had been tripped by Bibiji's premature departure. Stumbling to recover his balance, he must have drawn on the wisdom and discipline she had practised. I needed to discover that part of her legacy. Now that he was gone, my only hope was to seek it out in his surviving siblings.

Perhaps the most alchemic gift that she had bestowed on him was to illustrate by her passing the impermanence of every aspect of life, including life itself. It reminded me of what he would say in response to any trauma in my life.

'This too will pass.'

If he had arrived at this truth because of Bibiji's death, it was ironic that he did not speak explicitly of her, or of his determination that the value of her unfulfilled life should not be wasted. Some wounds run so deep that they defy the reach of words. Perhaps they require another medium to transcend the transience of life and the utter unavoidability of death. Once I put the conundrum of my father's singular serenity in his later years in that way, I saw that there was only one answer, a hopelessly flamboyant one at that, which eviscerated the cynicism of despair.

I had to laugh.

He had left me a clue on that walk around the reservoir. As he spoke, I caught his eyes looking over the water to a horizon I couldn't see. The lightness and depth with which he had stridden through Kabir's verses had made me falter involuntarily. He had chuckled, and imperceptibly pulled me closer, beyond death.

My father's passing in 1989 changed my life in a manner that he despaired of ever seeing. His death left in its wake unexpected responsibilities, forcing me off an unconventional path. I had spent nearly a decade with philanthropic organisations working with poor, rural communities and travelling across East, West and Southern Africa, to the increasing bewilderment of a father whose journey had been in the other direction, away from poverty. He saw my volunteerism as an indulgence at his expense; a waste of his investment in my education.

Within days of his funeral, his vision for me – or perhaps it was his memory of Bibiji's aspirations for her hungry children – was realised. I had fully entered Grihasta, the worldly 'householder' phase of a Hindu's life: I turned professional, traded casuals for suits, moved cities to be in Birmingham near my mother in her sudden widowhood, and bought a property two doors down from her. That set the scene for the scripted life I lived for the next decade and a half. I married – and divorced – worked obsessively, and travelled incessantly with projects across the globe.

I went to India often during this period, spurred by an obscure longing. But my visits invariably took the form of professional assignments to states unconnected to my ancestral roots. I would stop in Delhi to change planes, or for short briefing meetings with clients at their headquarters in the capital, before moving south or east to work in Andhra Pradesh, Gujarat, Karnataka, Kerala, Uttar Pradesh and West Bengal. Yet every time I returned to India I would hear the whispers more sharply from the north – summonses that were futile as I answered instead to the call of Maya, driven by alpha-male compulsions to excel professionally, and grow a successful consulting business.

It wasn't until 2005 that I properly resumed my quest for Bibiji, and this time the search would begin in England. In October 2005, I felt ready, and I was different. I had withdrawn from my business interests and had remarried with a quieter heart, exchanging vows in the dappled shade of a wild fig tree in the Lowveld of Limpopo. I had also become a father, blessed with two daughters, Radha Maud and Aditi Laxmi. They had arrived after I had crossed fifty, the age at which a Hindu should start disengaging from worldly entrapments. Both girls carried names inspired by my grandmothers, maternal and paternal. This journey would be as much for them as for me. I did not wish to leave them with rootless labels of identity.

The eldest of Bibiji's surviving children was living in north London. He was 87 and in poor health. I found him in a windowless 'granny' flat that had been converted unofficially, so that, from the outside, it still retained its appearance as a garage attached to his son's mansion.

A luxury BMW SUV was parked in the driveway. My uncle was sitting motionless, sunken into a turquoise leather sofa where the car would once have been. He received me with an ambivalent wave – the flourish of an out-turned palm, greeting and dismissing me in the same movement. I had telephoned ahead to say that I wanted to talk about his mother. In his better days, after my father's death, he would meet me with the deportment of the eldest uncle.

'How are you my son? In good health? Is your mother well? And work?'

Now we sat in silence. He stared at me, blinking periodically with big eyes and drooping eyelids. There was a moment when a flicker crossed his eyes. I thought then that the wall of silence that he had built around himself was about to break, and that his memories would pour out. But then the light faded from his eyes.

He turned his back and gestured to his deaf wife that he wanted to go to bed. I watched him crumple onto the mattress, his thin bones and pallid skin covered in white *kurta*-pyjamas. There was an air about him that suggested he was so close to the final frontier that he saw no point in writing narratives on water.

It made me think of the vitality with which my father had lived and died.

'He went out like a light,' the doctor had said of the exploding artery in my father's head. My eyes returned to my uncle. I could see him through the narrow passage that divided the garage into two rooms. His wife had placed a white cotton bed sheet over his still body and he had turned his face to the wall. I slipped out through the side exit into the garden. There was green everywhere; a cricket field adjoining the house and a farm opposite, across a quiet English country road. I savoured the taste of oxygen, thinking of the sinuous journey my uncle had taken to arrive here after leaving home and Bibiji at the age of 16.

He had crossed land and sea, and then land again, to reach Uganda in 1934 with the neatly inscribed address of a kinsman from Bajwara in hand. Soon after that he had moved to a weather station in rural Kenya, to record rainfall, noting the contents of collection cones twice a day. It was there that he proved that Bibiji's training in tables and mathematics could take him further than just writing numbers. He found his vocation as an accountant, first with the colonial service's post office, then as a school bursar and finally as a commercial accountant. Throughout his active working life he had always maintained two jobs at the same time: a full-time day job and an evening freelance accountancy service. He finally retired at 82.

I remembered a conversation I had had with him a few years earlier, before he had moved his family to this house. He told me of the fortune he had accumulated.

'It's mostly offshore in Jersey, away from the British taxman.'

I wanted to ask him if he had ever been there, the closest holiday destination over the sea from England, but held back out of respect for an elder who didn't believe in Sundays.

I walked back from the bottom of the garden past neatly trimmed shrubs and weedless borders. My cousin sat with his sons watching a satellite television sports channel on a plasma TV. I wasn't invited in. But I returned a few weeks later as a pallbearer to carry my uncle's coffin out of the house.

A few months later, I flew to Delhi. India too – or at least metropolitan India – had visibly changed. It was flirting with the new theology that had swept the world in the 1980s and 1990s. The muezzin call of this new god of the market filled the air as we landed at Delhi airport. It came from the whining engines of European and North American carriers, and from India's smart new private airlines, Sahara and

Jet Airlines. I had flown Virgin, but not alone. I had come to trace Bibiji with the best Hindi-speaking research assistant I could find: my 73-year-old mother.

We walked off the plane together. My mother's tiny frame, all of four foot ten when we had departed from London, had shrivelled further in the dry air of the plane. Now she began to grow. In the days to come I would see her walk tall through the alleys of her childhood, giggling like a little girl as she was stopped by the hugs of anonymous women. She had spent less than eight years in the village of Apra in northern India before being taken to Kenya, but I could see that the imprint of that period was as indelible on her as the stain of Makupa was on me.

We entered Delhi airport to the familiar waft of India, but there was also another, fresher scent: the aroma of globalisation. The effect was jarring. This mixing of vapours had shaken off pieces of the old socialist garb of Indira Gandhi International Airport without completing the transition to modernity. The floors of the airport were now of white marble, not the flawless white of the temples and tombs of feudal times, but that streaked grey-white of the kitchens and bathrooms of the sub-continent's nouveau riche. Industrial floor tiles and carpeting covered the walkways, but were edged by thin ribbons of grime. Batteries of bright strip lights illuminated the passages and halls, but there was always at least one tube that was not properly aligned. TV monitors relayed up-to-date information on flight arrivals and departures, while exposed electrical cabling sagged into a cluttered socket mottled with the drip of successive coats of paint. A missing overhead ceiling panel revealed dust and cobwebs moulded into grotesque Tamil masks hanging off air ducts.

An escalator creaked between two floors, narrow, steep and symbolic; it could carry only a fortunate few between the strata that India was in a hurry to traverse. Everywhere the impression was of a battle over the facades of progress led by people who had seen Bangkok, Kuala Lumpur and Singapore, and wanted Delhi to go there.

I saw a sign for the toilets. A cleaner was mopping the floor, not on his hands and knees, but with a long handled brush. He wore the uniform of the new global caste of loo-cleaners: long dark trousers and matching short sleeved shirt, like the Bangladeshi in Dubai, the Turk in Frankfurt and the Zimbabwean in Cape Town. Only he looked skinnier and happier. His frame spoke of subsisting in India and his aura of freedom from xenophobia.

'How are you?' I asked in Hindi, using the respectful 'you'.

'I'm fine, absolutely fine,' he replied, his head rolling from side to side to accentuate the 'yes'. I knew I was now truly in India; it would take more than emergent collaborative ventures between Bollywood and Hollywood to change that gesture to a hip nod and a cool yes.

The urinals and basins smelt of phenol, bleach and diabetic urine. The cleaner didn't ask for a tip, and his generous smile troubled my conscience. But not enough to make me part with one of my hundred rupee notes. I was taken aback by the artless parsimony with which I was already calibrating a tip appropriate to India. I justified my meanness with the thought that I didn't have any ten or fifty rupee notes. In fact, I was carrying very little cash in any currency; my money was encoded on a plastic chip.

I joined my mother and we walked into a spacious foyer with evenly spaced, paired cubicles for immigration officers. A hand-painted sign invited complaints to a supervisor. The geometry and the message on the sign reminded me of Johannesburg airport, but without the glitz of the City of Gold. I wondered again why this peculiar design, funnelling arrivals towards clenched sluice gates controlled by paired officers, had become so ubiquitous in modern, international airports. Was this about fostering peer pressure and efficiency in processing passports? Or was there something deliberately more ominous in this imagery, indicative of a deeper fear? Of a world increasingly awash with floods of migrants, that needed to be controlled more tightly, with barriers and doubled authority, leaving absolutely no touch or space for the natural human impulse for hospitality?

The last possibility provoked an unexpectedly vicarious and malign thought. Nine out of ten passengers around me were Indian and most were queuing with the impatience of people returning home. The rest were virtually all white, and they bristled with an ambivalent energy. Many looked like they were meeting the smell of India for the first time and it had stirred fear, inhibiting the desire to begin their adventure. My pulse quickened. I wanted to see the nervous whites treated badly, like Africans and Indians arriving in Europe. I looked over at the immigration officers and willed them to demonstrate that India too had found its voice in this ungenerous new world.

I felt no embarrassment even when I reflected that this malice defaced the humanity of my English wife and mixed race children. But it made me look around again. There was only one black African in any of the queues. I recognised her as the Nigerian beautician on the Virgin Airlines flight we had just come off. I wanted to talk to her – share my spite, exhibit my knowledge of the similarities between this half-cooked airport and Lagos, reveal to her my claims to African-ness amid the multiple identities and allegiances I now carried so adeptly. But she moved on quickly through the crew channel, throwing a smile at me that spoke of waking up in Africa.

It was our turn to hand over our passports. The immigration officer examined our five-year multiple entry visas, a privilege for those with Indian ancestry. His gaze softened faintly in greeting. I took the liberty of leaning against his wooden counter while talking to my mother, an act unthinkable in Europe, while he swiped the electronic strip and completed the formalities.

He checked my face. I had carried a British passport for over twenty years. In all that time I had never entered England without my stomach in a knot, my jaw tightening to the impassive scrutiny of eyes that moved from Her Majesty's paper to trace the lines of my coloured skin. Now, here I was with that same face, my ancestry apparent in its contours, my Indian mother by my side. The officer rolled his head; that same sideways movement that I would struggle to resist copying while in India. I collected my passport and went through, free of the shadow of rejection. This was like crossing the threshold into a grandmother's home.

We walked into a large open customs-and-baggage hall with conveyor belts. A few officers were standing by two clearly marked 'green' and 'red' exits. Alert and unobtrusive, they watched as passengers walked past pushing trolleys and wheeling Samsonites. Urban India had replaced another caste without remark. I wondered where the coolies had gone to die.

A series of posters emblazoning the theme 'Incredible India' hung from just below the ceiling of the hall. They had the middle-class confidence and self-deprecating humour of a country confident that it could hold its own in the zeitgeist of this consumptive age. My eyes settled on two posters. I didn't concern myself overly with the photographs on them: a solitary climber in the infinity of the Himalayas and a white water rafter in one of the many churning rivers that feed the Ganges. The pictures were for the blind. It was the captions underneath that told the unchanging truth about India.

'How to turn into a dot,' said the first.

'Don't panic; there's always a rebirth,' said the second.

Three of Bibiji's surviving children lived in Delhi. I went in search of the youngest, the former bank manager from Kapurthala. Or rather, I went looking for a register.

Bapu had kept a record of the family's land transactions in a book in which he had, apparently, from time to time, also noted other matters of consequence: births, deaths and dues. This log would have passed with the family's assets to the inheritor of Bapu's estate. I was looking for the uncle who had taken possession of the agricultural land in the fields around Bajwara and the ancestral house in the village itself. It was there that that I had seen a large trunk of books and parchments in 1972. I had leafed gingerly through the papers and school books on top of the pile, fingering the yellow crumbling paper on which Bibiji's light had shone to guide her children out of the intractable poverty that had been her curse. I was hoping that somewhere below, past the upper layer of papers that had arrested my search more than three decades ago, there might have been a log – or notes or other forms of evidence in some legible form – recording the transactions Bibiji had undertaken to support the family.

The anecdotes I had collected over the years revealed an enterprising woman. Right up to the time she died, she had kept two cows in the backyard to maintain an unbroken supply of milk for her children. She had sold the surplus milk to neighbours to sustain an independent trickle of income. In the afternoons, she had given private tuition to the children of richer families, sitting her own children down at the same time, thereby ensuring that their inviolable study time brought money as well as freedom from Bapu's vagaries. She made yogurt daily and regularly sent out bowls to the families of the doctor, the headmaster, the teachers and army officers, to ensure reciprocal favours in times of need.

The impression that had emerged was of a woman who had meticulously constructed each rung of the ladder with the clarity of a captive sizing up the walls of her prison. I was eager to see if – and how – Bapu had recorded this project.

We went in search of my uncle's house, my mother insisting on a three-wheeler auto-rickshaw rather than a regular Ambassador cab.

She said it was easier to stop and ask for directions unimpeded by the doors and windows of a car, adding, 'Why waste money? A car won't get us there any faster.'

Twenty minutes later, in that broad frontier between old and New Delhi where the intersections become choke points, we were idling in the fumes of a traffic jam. A dark woman in her twenties with long, uncombed black hair and gleaming white teeth, wearing a grimy orange sari approached us. She had a baby slung around her hip and had in tow a child of six or seven years old. Beneath the mask of a mournful scowl she looked healthier than Anil, our anaemic, saddle-bound, auto-rickshaw driver. She swung her baby towards my face and begged in a croaky voice

'Sahib, the children are hungry. Give me some money for food.'

My mother, sitting on the other side of the bench-seat, leaned forward, turned sideways across me to confront the woman directly. She spoke to the woman as easily and naturally as she had done a moment earlier, when conversing with Anil the driver about his family.

'You should be ashamed of yourself. You are a mother. What are you teaching your children? Go work.' The woman walked away with her children, completely unabashed. Anil wobbled his head, equally unfussed.

It was an Abyssinian moment: old, layered and ambiguous. In Addis Ababa it had been the cab driver who had expressed a larger, laconic view on this conundrum: on the impulse to help versus the possibility that the seeds of poverty lie in the gifts of charity. I had been traveling in a decrepit old Fiat taxi then. We were stuck at the traffic lights approaching Revolution Square – since renamed Meskel Square to drop the association with the brutal era of the Derg regime. A middle-aged bedraggled man in grey trousers and a soiled tweed jacket had approached my side of the car. He looked like a character from the

lower ranks of the Imperial Palace, someone who had fallen out of
the pages of Kapuscinski's 'Emperor', that elegant account of the fall
of Haile Selassie. The man had stretched out his hand wordlessly, in
that same universal petition for alms. Then too, I had felt awkward.
I was on my way to the World Bank office. Tadesse, the cab driver,
stared at me, and waving the man away, asked: 'What do you expect
when our leaders go begging for foreign aid?'

We found my uncle in Malviya Nagar in southern Delhi, on the
third floor of a building indistinguishable from any other in a maze
of concrete tenements. It had taken an hour to find an apartment
that was less than fifty metres off a major road. All around, in every
narrow pot-holed alley, packed with the tinny boxcars that now
defined middle-class India, buildings were growing in the only way
they could: up towards the sky.

This uncle too lived in his son's house. When we arrived, he was in
a room adjoining the lounge in which we met. This sitting room was
typical of the many in which I would be entertained on this trip: a
newish TV; long, shiny, dark table and six chairs with high backs
and plasticky upholstery; very pale blue walls hung with pictures of
Hanuman and Mata, and a copper plate with an Om sign over the
Gayatri Mantra; a low, handcrafted settee and matching armchairs,
tossed with cotton cushions in the colours and motifs of mangoes
and almonds – pale yellows, creamy browns and shades of green.
And, as always, no books in sight.

A thin, short male nurse wheeled my uncle into our presence. My
uncle was slouched in a wheelchair, speechless, partially paralysed
and incontinent from a stroke that he had suffered nine years before.
Tubes and translucent bags hung off him. He stared at us – again
those big eyes – and then, as he recognised my mother and me, his
shoulders heaved with the happy abandon of an autistic child. He

let out sounds of delight, and then was stuck in a guttural repetitive loop unable to form words. It was an affecting reunion. I had never forgotten our first and only other encounter days after I had heard that I would be going to university. Bapu had whispered this news into his ear, and his immediate response had been celebratory.

Now he just looked at me, and unable to communicate further, he subsided into a foetal lump, enveloped by a blank silence. My aunt and the nurse set to work on him together, while my mother asked questions about him as if he were not there. The carers pushed and shifted his body, lessening the arc and rearranging his torso, legs, arms, shoulders and head until he was settled in the wheelchair like a wide-eyed rag doll on a child's pram. From this posture, he maintained a grip on me with a vacant gaze.

I flinched at the scene before me. Another hope-filled human life was coming to a close. But I was aware that I shared more than just this philosophical space, this universal human predicament, with him. Before me was a man from the same nest as my father. His trajectory personified for me the harshness – and the incomprehensibility – of a particular kind of life in India which had led him from rural poverty to a grinding competitive struggle for survival through the sunless alleyways and artless rooms of small-town northern India to raise a family, and then ultimately to this capital sentence. While he was assiduously, single-mindedly making his way up through the vaulted storeys of the Bank of Patiala, I was growing up to the open expanses and wildernesses of Tsavo, Masai Mara and Serengeti; dancing to Prince Nico Mbarga's Hi-Life and Fela's Afro-jazz with African friends whose mother-tongues I could not speak, but who invariably called me 'brother'; walking my dogs, Patchy and Toothache, in the aloe-sprinkled slopes of the hills of Hhohho that fed the headwaters of the Umbuluzi; and slowly, inexorably, being drawn into clandestine support for an armed struggle for the liberation of a country which hadn't even existed in the school books of my childhood.

I saw that I had been the beneficiary of a fortuitous current of destiny that had carried my parents to Kenya and brought my soul to life in Africa. It mattered not that the star-filled skies and dead authors whose company kept me awake into the night would care little of my life's passing, nor that I might leave less of a mark on this world than my uncle had. I was simply grateful for the life I had been given and the aesthetics and sensibilities that shaped me.

Once my uncle had been settled in his room, we sat for lunch. I asked my aunt about her daughter – her other child, a cousin I remembered with affection. She had been a coy, little girl of about three or four when I had last visited.

'Oh Rosie, she did a PhD. Got a gold star. She's a teacher – and gives tuition and writes science text books in her spare time.'

Perhaps that was what my uncle had been trying to tell me through the barrier of scrambled neuro-synapses when he had seen me. Yet another strand of the family tree had produced a doctor. Bibiji's eight surviving children had produced 28 grandchildren, all of whom had 'made good' educationally and professionally; most with multiple degrees and doctorates, covering disciplines that read like an index on a campus map: Accountancy and Commerce; Anthropology; Biological Sciences; Computer Sciences, Dentistry; Economics; Education; English Literature; Fine Arts; Law; Management and Business Administration; Mathematics; Mechanical Engineering; Medicine; Pharmacy; Organisational Development; Physics; Psychology; and Sociology. Within this group, more women than men had doctorates. Or perhaps more of the genes that carried them to that title.

After the meal, my cousin, a handsome, fine-featured Soni who looked younger than his age of around 40, invited me up to the roof terrace of the tenement block. I remembered the moment, decades ago, when he had led the way to the open toilet on the terrace. He had been six or seven years old then. This time he led me to a room on the terrace, a squat structure of breezeblock. Almost every roof of the neighbouring tenements had a similar construction, with rusting air-conditioning units plumbed into their sides. Modern urban India was laid out before me. In every direction that I looked, white, silver and grey satellite dishes were supplicating to the same point in the sky. Clusters of black water tanks were banked above every building to capture the irregular supply from the city's supply pipes, which flowed for only three to four hours a day and had to meet an ever increasing demand from the growing population of people, flush toilets and washing machines. Legal and illegal electrical and telephone cables tangled and stretched in every direction, with the anarchic randomness of an infant's scribbles running to the very edge of a page. A crow landed on the far terrace wall and strode jerkily along the parapet, like an unwound mechanical toy, before turning its head aristocratically to look at us.

My cousin ushered me into his rooftop cell. It was his 'home office'. He settled like a tycoon on his swivelling office chair. The shelves behind him were littered with bits and pieces of the broken fax machines from his repair-and-maintenance business. He told me that his business had declined and was dying with the arrival of the Internet and personal computers. His tools were laid out neatly in a tray on the desk. Diwali was a week away, and he had them ready for the annual *puja*. The pundit was due in a day or two to bless the implements of his livelihood.

I brought the conversation back to the purpose of my visit: my interest in any papers and records from the past, and in whether he could share any information about our grandmother. He answered the question with a frown. 'What trunk? There were some pots and pans, and linen. We gave them to the Dhantee's family. That's what Bapu had said we should do. *Thayi* cleared the house after that. If there were any papers left around, she probably threw them away.'

Then he added: 'Did you know that I was with Bapu when he died? He asked to be cremated at the same spot as Bibiji.'

If true, it was an astonishing statement of sentimentality and loyalty from Bapu towards Bibiji. The theatrics disturbed me, not fitting with my experience of Bapu. And Bapu aside, such memorial symmetry felt alien to the way Hindus think of death and funereal arrangements. It brought back to mind a question that had agitated me through all the years during which I had reflected on the enigma of Bibiji's life, and my desire to find her, not only for myself, but also for my daughters who would likely grow up in an English culture without access to the other parts of their heritage: why were there so few biographies of, and memoirs by, 'ordinary' Indians?

Curiously, when I began my search for Bibiji, I had looked for biographies of Indian Hindu grandmothers, much as a white Zimbabwean might seek stories of Scottish Presbyterian grandmothers. I had found only three books: Mira Kamdar's *Motiba's Tattoos: A Granddaughter's Journey into Her Indian Family's Past*; Broughton Coburn's story about his adopted Nepalese Hindu grandmother, *Aama in America*; and Parita Mukta's *Shards of Memory*. Kamdar describes herself as an American with part East-Indian ancestry; Broughton is an American who lived briefly in Nepal; Mukta sees herself as British with a Kenyan-Indian past. None of these three put Indian or Hindu as the first descriptor of their variegated identity.

It was odd to find such a hole in Indian literature, in a culture with a love for stories and centuries of written poetry, folk tales and scripture. The puzzle was solved on a tennis court in Hatfield, Pretoria. I had finished playing with Shankar, a friend who was the military attaché to the Indian Embassy. As we sat in the winter sun, our conversation had drifted to current preoccupations. I had asked him if he knew of any such books.

'We don't build mausoleums to the dead,' he responded.

He was right, of course. There are no gravestones and there is no tradition of eulogies in Hindu culture. Clothes and personal artefacts of the dead are given away to the poor. Jewellery is seldom retained;

it is smelted and recast, or sold. I remembered that my maternal grandmother's bangles had reincarnated as an aunt's bangles in a new design.

What then is biography when a person's life is seen as a continuous 'karmic' journey, a soul migrating fluidly through countless forms and cycles? As I pondered on the 'biographical' aspects of the Hindu stories that I could recall, I saw that the emphasis was on understanding the moral principle, the *dharmic* quality of a person's life – not the glory or otherwise of a one-off human act.

My cousin's claim that Bapu had asked for his body to be burnt at the same spot 38 years on from where Bibiji was cremated would have made my father guffaw. Everyone is cremated at the same place anyway. The smoke goes into the ether, and the ashes into running water. No markers remain of a life returning to Life. I wanted to laugh too, but it felt disrespectful to the only grandson to walk with Bapu in the last years of our grandfather's life, and the one who had performed the final rites.

We left the house. Outside, by the Hanuman temple, a mendicant in orange robes was sitting on the steps of a cyber café eating rice and dhal from a plate moulded out of dried pressed leaves. He paused to peer closely at this food through thick lenses in black plastic frames, plucked out a curry leaf, and let it drop onto the fragmenting, littered roadside. His spectacles reminded me of an Irish friend's remark made as we dug water pipes alongside women and men from a rural community near Mbekelweni, in the Lutfonja Hills of Swaziland.

'You need good eyes to look through glasses like that,' Peter had said to an old *uBabaMkulu*, who had come to watch us labour. That day, after packing our tools, we had sat silently on a crop of rocks to watch the dying light of the African sun. Young boys had passed below us, prodding their cows back to kraals over yet another mountain.

Here too the sun was setting. The bazaar was coming alive. Bright naked bulbs dangled outside shops and kiosks. Workers were pausing on their way home, held by the pangs of love and duty to buy glistening cucumbers to add to the evening meal, two more red and gold plastic bangles for the family princess, henna shampoo to add shine to the hair of the beloved.

Two young boys, around ten or twelve years old, in white cricket kits with their bats in hand, were walking through plumes of diesel. I hadn't seen a blade of grass all day and yet they quickened my heart to the promise of another pair like Laxman and Dravid. As youngsters, they too must have walked home like this in the fading Indian light, instinctively, playfully swinging their bats, unaware that fate would write them into sporting history for overthrowing an imperious Australian cricketing era against impossible odds and with unimaginable artistry.

Bibiji's second youngest child had been ten when she died. He was now a fit 71 years old. I found him living in yet another lower middle class 'colony' in south Delhi. He had added two floors to his original one-floor apartment. The result was a higgledy-piggledy collection of rooms hanging off a jagging internal stairwell. When we had last met a mood of anger surrounded him, fired by the bitterness of being a late child in a family with resources that couldn't stretch beyond the education of the early arrivals. Now, I found mellowness suffused with softer memories. His wife had recently returned from extended stays in America and England where three of their four children were now living, and the couple had settled into a habit of living in different rooms.

I retreated with him to his bedroom with tea that he made without any fuss, while my mother kept my aunt company elsewhere in the house. His room was plainly furnished. A lightly patterned off-white bed sheet covered the hard mattress on the wooden bed on which we sat. There was no headboard. Two white pillows brushed against a whitewashed wall. A still white fan hung overhead. The window looked out onto another concrete tenement block across the narrow dusty road I had come along.

'So, what do you want to know from me?' my uncle asked. His tone was kind.

'Tell me about Bibiji; what she looked like, her voice...'

He didn't let me finish. It was as if, acute to the early passing of my father's life, and aware of his own mortality, he had a testimony to give; that his story of his mother needed to be heard.

He sat upright, his eyes intent, and spoke unhesitatingly as if the vision was absolutely clear in his mind. He mixed Punjabi, Hindi and English, with the English sentences moulded into a structure that came from the first two.

'She was tall and fair and had straight hair,' he began. 'She wore Punjabi suits, *salwar-kameezes*, and saris only occasionally. She had very simple earrings and one bangle – only one bangle. She wore glasses when she read. They came from Hoshiarpur.

'All the clothes in the family were sewn by her. Bapu's too. She taught in the local primary school and also offered tuition at home – some classes for free. She was always working – from before we woke up until after we went to sleep.'

His mother had died more than 60 years ago, but in his voice still flexed to the tug of awe and anger at the conditions in which Bibiji had lived. It was the first time that a living picture of Bibiji took form in my mind.

I asked again about her voice. I wanted to know the source of my father's singing voice, which had been captured in an anonymous recording by a travelling radio-journalist and played on All India Radio.

'Bibiji had a sweet voice, and she sang while she did the housework – *bhajans* and patriotic songs. She would speak often of the country being free one day. I remember one song that she sang often:

"Let Bhagat Singh be my groom;

Let Hari Kishen be my best man."

'Should I make some more tea? Have some of the *balushahi*,' he added, pointing to the plate of sweets I hadn't touched. 'They're really tasty, son.'

He returned with more tea, my aunt following. I promised her that I would eat properly later, but wanted to talk to my uncle longer. He wobbled his head as she left, and smiled conspiratorially at the prerogative of the visitor. There was new warmth to his voice as he spoke again.

'Bibiji was kind as nobody can be. She offered food to whoever came home, no matter how little we had. And no *sadhu* or *fakir* could go from the door without his alms bowl filled. She would say, "Do good; that's religion! And do your own work." Everyone had to have a wash and pray in the morning. We all recited the *Gayatri Mantra*. She gave top priority to education and cleanliness, and ours was one of the first houses in the village to have a dry latrine. She had it built.'

He went quiet for a while, making space for me to write notes. I looked out of the window. Three rooms were lit up in the block opposite. They were splayed like open, unfilled boxes in a crossword puzzle. Lights with no shades, just naked bulbs, illuminated them. A middle-aged man with a potbelly in a white sleeveless vest and a chequered blue lungi walked through one of the rooms oblivious to my voyeurism.

My uncle resumed, 'She was very affectionate, except when she sat us down for studies. Then she was very strict. She would swear and say that if we failed, we were doomed. There would be no fees for a repeat year. And that education was our only hope.'

This was the same condition that my father had imposed on my siblings and me: one strike and you are out. Then my uncle's tone changed. There was a sharper energy, a recollection of justice served. 'She would call out all our names in one breath, and sit us in a line with our books. And also like that at mealtimes. In the morning and at night, everyone got the same amount of milk. We would drink milk and *lassi* – never tea. No tea. She cooked the best *saag*, and made the best *kheer*. Nobody could make *saag* like Bibiji. At Diwali, she would make *barfi*.'

The images were strung together like invocations in a love song that he was accustomed to singing to himself through sadder times.

'She became sick three days before she died. On the first evening, she asked your father to fetch Dr Mulk Raj Bhasin. She had faith in him. We all had faith in him. Even if he gave us mud, it worked.'

Your father returned and said that Dr Bhasin had gone to Lahore and would be back in two or three days. She immediately went into a coma. She was waiting for Ram Pal to come before she died. He was her favourite son. He was studying at DAV College in Lahore. As soon as he came, she opened her eyes, and then she died.'

He was looking directly at me. His face was still, with unwavering big brown eyes. We sat quietly for a few moments. Then he added, 'She planted an orchard, but saw no fruit.'

The questions of a lifetime jostled before me. Instead, I asked about Bapu.

'He was very cruel. He slept alone. Bibiji slept with us. We would all lie in a row – all the boys. And Bibiji would sleep by the door. Bapu would yell in the middle of the night and ask her to bring water. And then he would hit her – slap her and shout that she had brought it late.'

My aunt came into the room. My uncle and I both knew that our private time was over. There was no time to talk further about domestic violence, and it was unnecessary. I had heard from my mother of my father's recollections of Bapu's conduct, which he had revealed to her in rare moments of disclosure. Bapu would come home, after gambling, or feuding, and string the boys from the rafters and lash them with rope. Or he would take pleasure in pinning their young hands or feet under the corner posts of a *charpoy*, as punishment for a whimsically adjudged misdemeanour. There was psychological abuse too, though it would probably not have been seen as such in those stoutly patriarchal days. I'd heard about Bapu eating meat in a household of vegetarians, and doing so before a young family watching in hunger. But my father had never directly spoken of Bapu's assaults on Bibiji. Perhaps the wounds had never healed, or the shame was too great. Or perhaps, like others fleeing the land of their birth, he had let such memories go, releasing them into the sea on his first voyage to Kenya.

I had heard more about Bibiji in an hour than I had gathered in weeks. Her form began to sharpen, and then, perversely, to heighten my scepticism. I considered the nature of memory. What had 61 years of loss, retelling and repression done with images burnt into the heart of my uncle, a child bereaved at ten?

He had described Bibiji in images that were irresistible. Perhaps that is exactly what they were. I had yet to meet a Punjabi who didn't believe his mother made the best *saag* or *kheer*. Even the presence of the revolutionary Bhagat Singh in the narrative threatened the security of my gains.

Bhagat Singh was an independence fighter who was driven by the massacre at Jallianwala Bagh. He was hanged in March 1931 in Lahore by the British government. Bibiji was 34 years old when this historic event took place, not in some distant part of India, but in the capital of her native state of Punjab. This uncle was born five years later in 1936. So the likelihood of Bibiji singing eulogies to Bhagat Singh in the 1940s, the time from which my uncle's memories would have stemmed, was credible.

Indian nationalism, like most popular liberation movements, had effectively galvanised public sentiment through poetry and song, to counter legislative inequality and state violence. And women – especially relatively educated women like Bibiji – had played a key, if largely invisible, role in the struggle for freedom. They had put the freedom of the country before challenging the quiescent conditions of inequality within their own society. Given Bibiji's singing voice and her longstanding involvement with the progressive Arya Samaj, the songs that underpinned the nationalist movement would have been very familiar to her.

But were there brushstrokes of melodrama in my uncle's rendition? There had been seven popular Hindi movies on the life and martyrdom of Bhagat Singh, including Manoj Kumar's classic, *Shaheed*, in 1965, which it was almost impossible not to have seen, and two blockbusters in 2002; Ajay Devgun's *The Legend of Bhagat Singh* and Sunny Deol's *23 March 1931: Shaheed*. Every one of these films, and indeed most Bollywood patriotic films, has this image of 'ordinary' Punjabi or Indian women doing their laundry against a backdrop of nationalistic sacrifice – with no oppressive husbands in sight, of course.

Aside from these films, there was an unending stream of books and articles on Bhagat Singh, mostly in Hindi, but also in English. The Indian public's fascination with the story of this remarkable idealist appeared to have grown in proportion to people's disillusionment with post-independence politicians. My uncle, an avid reader of this genre, could easily have re-choreographed his memories of Bibiji borrowing iconic images freely from these sources.

I let these reservations pass. If the songs were an embellishment, then they were an acceptable one. After all, in India every modern telling of an epic requires at least a song and usually also a dance. Most of what my uncle had said rang true. It made me eager to hurry north.

I decided to do so with my aunt, Swaran Kanta, who was now the oldest survivor of Bibiji's nine children who'd grown to adulthood. There was something else that led me to this decision. My aunt had been physically present when Bibiji had passed on; and it was also in her presence that I had faced the news of my father's death. It was as if Death were signalling that the living lines of history flowed through Swaran Bua. I needed to hear her stories.

My mother too wanted to travel north, but she was being pulled by her own memories, and wanted to visit the village of her birth, Apra. We agreed to travel together. The road to Hoshiarpur passed through Jalandhar district, and Apra was a short tangent off the trunk road.

Swaran Bua lived in the quintessentially middle-class northern suburbs of New Delhi, across the holy River Yamuna. These are the heartlands of the Bharatiya Janata Party, the BJP of Hindu Nationalists. Their political control of Delhi had spawned yet another bridge across the river, and the doubling in size of the one I had previously taken to go north. There were now four lanes in each direction. The traffic was even slower. Buses, minibuses, cars, auto-rickshaws, motorbikes and scooters jostled with each other, inching their way through a viscous cloud of carbon.

Decades ago, I had seen domesticated elephants bathing in the river below. This time I saw a black bank of treacle, flanked by stacked terraces of mud, brick and tin shanties perched on the tiered banks. Water is the reason for Delhi's location on this bend in the Yamuna's meander through the Gangetic plains. But the river had become the drain into which the city's factory waste and domestic sewage flowed, with the certainty of gravity and middle-class economic growth. I had read local media reports of scientific studies stating that toxicity in the Yamuna was 100 000 times above the legal safety limits for human exposure by World Health Organisation standards. But such analyses seemed inconsequential to the Hindu pilgrims piling out of buses to dip into the waters and young boys frolicking in the shallows.

Perhaps it is the river itself that inspires an abandonment of fear. As my fume-spewing auto-rickshaw twisted its way between vehicles only millimetres apart, I looked past the faces of drivers and passengers as close as a reflection in a morning shaving mirror. There on the narrow pedestrian pathway on the side of the bridge overlooking the river was a vendor selling fruit and vegetables. A green-and-black freckled heap of custard apples caught my eye. Alongside them was a pile of glossy aubergines, onto which the vendor was flicking water to maintain the shine of freshness.

The rickshaw-*wallah* threaded his three-wheeler through the traffic at my behest. By the time we reached my aunt's house, I had blissfully made up for years of unfulfilled desire, having devoured more than a dozen custard apples. I cleaned my sticky hands on my freshly laundered trousers, wiped my face on my sleeve, and ascended to a state of gratitude for the slow traffic.

My aunt was waiting and her hug felt more maternal than ever before. There was a mellower, softer quality to the intimacy between her and my mother, textured by the gentleness of age. I showered quickly and returned to find that the housemaid had been left happily alone to prepare a simple vegetarian meal, while the two old women talked. Their conversation reflected precise, encyclopaedic knowledge of each other's family, and the sound of another epoch slipping away. The events in their sentences were instinctively referenced against the main festivals of the year, Maha Shivratri, Holi, Baisakhi, Ram Naumi, Rakhi, Krishan Janamastmi, Dussehra, Diwali – a calendar woven out of lunar and seasonal strands, and populated not by numbers, but by the stories and myths of Hindu gods. I could think of no contemporary who used this almanac.

I was shown into the same room in which I had been lying when news of my father's death had come, 18 years before. I furtively checked the curtains and bed sheets; they were similar, but not of the same brown-and-white pattern.

Fifteen to twenty years ago, in her prime, when her husband was a Session Court Judge and the mystique of his office had power over small people, my aunt had strode the stage haughtily. Then, she had cultivated an air of impatience and entitlement; her silk saris and intricately carved gold bangles expected to be heard immediately. Now I saw that his death ten years ago had not just embalmed her in the muted hues of widowhood. It had done what the death of a partner often does: it had lit up her frailties and qualities.

She was dressed plainly and there was an air of tenderness about her. She told me that she divided her time between Delhi and Shimla, with three seasons here and the burning summer months in Shimla. She was generally quieter and, at 77, healthier than she had been for years. She said that, with her children settled in their own nuclear families, she had found herself turning naturally to the study of yoga and acupressure, and that she worked as a volunteer therapist in a complementary health clinic in Delhi.

I saw Bibiji hovering over this picture. It brought to mind Zen Master Thich Nhat Hanh's words: 'When we liberate ourselves, we liberate our ancestors.' My aunt's story reached back into time and brought to life Bibiji's encoded messages to her children. She had dressed them in the guise of precepts for economic independence, but I sensed from my aunt's bearing that Bibiji had always known that the power of these injunctions was larger.

My aunt had broken generations of tradition to marry a man of her own choice, despite Bapu's objections. It had been a momentous scandal, impelling her from the village, but she had found a companion who never faltered in his intellectual respect and romantic affection for her. Yet her husband's death had not broken my aunt. The strength of her education – she had a Master's degree in Hindi Literature – and her business acumen meant that she lived comfortably off the properties she rented out in two cities.

Despite these vivid connections and legacies associated with Bibiji, I still anticipated that my aunt would be unwilling to talk about her mother. That is how it had always been, and though I had phoned ahead to tell her of the purpose of my visit, I thought I might need days of allusion and then persuasion to prise out buried memories. Instead, I found her ready with an array of facts and anecdotes, well organised thanks to the experience she had gained in working with her late husband when he had gone into private legal practice after retiring from the bench. It was as if her own immortality – the validity and power of her life story – depended on reincarnating a mother who had died 61 years ago.

We sat together on her bed. She sat cross-legged in her *salwar-kameeze*, half way down to allow me the comfort of leaning against the back wall and stretching out my legs. I faced an open door to a storeroom where a large, dark-brown wooden trunk with brass brackets was visible. She faced the door leading to the hallway where I had taken the call about my father's death.

She began slowly, decisively, like an old woman pouring the right measure of water on *atta*, and kneading the dough deftly for rotis.

'Bibiji was born in 1897 in the village of Baddowal, about 25 kilometres from Ludhiana, and about the same distance from our village near Hoshiarpur. She was the seventh child of her parents' nine children. She was named Lakshmi Devi because her birth coincided with good fortune in her father's life; he had secured a promotion around the time of her birth. Her father, a Bhandari, was an engineer in the Kingdom of Gwalior. Bibiji said he was an angry and violent man.

'She was four years old when she became engaged to Bapu. That was in 1901. There is a story behind how she came to marry Bapu.'

She paused, sensing the astonishment on my face.

'Bibiji had two older sisters. The oldest sister died within a year of her marriage. The next sister was then married to the same man. This sister, too, died within a year of marriage. When the family of the man, now twice bereaved, asked for the hand of the next Bhandari daughter, Bibiji's parents refused. That is how they came to marry their daughter to Bapu.

'Bapu was born in 1889 in Bajwara. He was the third son of a wealthy landowner.

Bibiji and Bapu were married in 1912. She was 15 and he was 23 at the time.

'Bibiji died at the age of 47 in 1946, after 32 years of marriage. For 25 of these years, from 1913 to 1938, she was either pregnant or breastfeeding. Her first child, a daughter, was born in 1914, and her last in 1938. She conceived 15 times altogether. She had four miscarriages and gave birth to 11 children. Two of the 11 children she gave birth to died in their infancy, one after six months, the other after 18 months. Nine of us children survived to adulthood. Your father, Rajinder, was the fifth of the nine children.'

My aunt stopped and turned to a hardback folder beside her. It was covered with patterned purple-and-red printed paper, rather like a school notebook, dressed up to bring cheer and individuality in the face of the sameness of grey mediocrity. She took out from it a sheet of paper on which she had composed a neat list, and handed it to me. She had laboured to put it in English for me, and it demonstrated a mathematical crispness of which her mother would have approved.

1914	Daughter, Savitri. First child. Savitri died in 1973.
1915–17	Two miscarriages.
1918	Son, Yashbir Chand.
1919–21	Two children born. One died after six months, the other after 18 months.
1921–24	Two more miscarriages.
1925	Son, Ram Pal. Died 1950. Poisoned to death.
1928	Daughter, Swaran Kanta (me).
1930	Son, Rajinder Pal. Died in 1989 – your father.
1932	Son, Raj Pal.
1934	Son, Krishan Gopal.
1936	Son, Vijay Pal.
1938	Son, Jatinder Pal.

We sat in silence for a while as she gave me time to assimilate the bare facts of Bibiji's life. Then, as if moved by a spirit she hadn't anticipated, she rose from the bed and walked to the storeroom. I saw her move ironed laundry and towels stacked on top of the trunk, lift its heavy top and dig deep into its recesses. She walked back to the bed slowly, serenely, and removed a small folded package wrapped in paper from a plastic carrier bag. Each movement was slow and meditative. As she unwrapped the paper, I saw it contained a cloth. She unfolded the cloth and placed it between us.

'Son, have this.'

It was a rectangular piece of village cotton-khaddar, 26 by 35 centimetres – about the size of the screen of a large laptop. The cloth was in two colours: an outside 'frame' of indigo along the four sides, about three centimetres wide, enclosing an inner area in brown. The slight melding of the two colours along the lines where they met suggested that the pattern was the result of tie dying. At the centre of the cloth was the symbol for Om embroidered using more than 300 tiny glass beads, each bead about a millimetre in diameter. The Om was ringed on three sides – all but the top – by a laurel of embroidered leaves and flowers. The pronounced stem and emboldened leaves had been created from several layers of stitching and crocheting in yellow-green thread. The flowers were made from elliptical, curved mother-of-pearl buttons. Each leaf was about two-to-three centimetres long and each flower about three-to-four centimetres. The laurel had been meticulously embroidered to ensure that the Om sat within an arrangement of perfect symmetry.

'Bibiji made this when I was about eight. I have kept it safe ever since.'

I picked it up gingerly. Bibiji had stitched it over 70 years ago, probably as she was watching over her elder children studying, and breastfeeding her penultimate child after her fifteenth pregnancy. When else would she have found the time to conceive the design and craft this creation so meticulously? Where did she get the money for the mother-of-pearl buttons? What made her create something so beautiful in the midst of poverty? What message was she weaving into a piece that would only be displayed in the next millennium, by a grandson born on a continent beyond her imagination?

We stopped for lunch – typical, delicious Punjabi fare: *maa ki daal* (black lentils), *bhindi* (okra or lady's fingers), plain yogurt and fresh *chapatis*, with a side salad of sliced onions, tomatoes and green chillies. My aunt ate with the same silence and Zen-like concentration that my father would bring to meals: no past, no future, just the taste of the present. And then, as soon as the last drop of water had been drunk from the steel tumbler, she was animated again. 'Come on, let's carry on.'

I smiled at the sacrifice of her afternoon nap. We returned to her room, and she resumed: 'Bibiji was tall; as tall as Savitri's daughter, your cousin, Sneh. (That would have made her around 5 foot, 4 inches. I made an accompanying note in my journal that Sneh was Bibiji's first and eldest granddaughter.) And she had the same build and complexion; slim and fair, like Sneh. She had slightly prominent upper front teeth. Her hair was grey and white when I was a child, but completely white by the time she died. She had big eyes, and wore spectacles for reading. She never used cosmetics of any kind – not even henna or *desi* (traditional) ayurvedic herbal lotions.' She emphasised the last point; it was clearly of interest to my aunt, who was a keen advocate of the Ayurvedic School.

'Your grandmother was a very intelligent and educated woman, and very hard working. She completed her Ratan (A levels/college entrance exams) and Bhushan (degree/postgraduate studies) after marriage. Both of these were in Hindi literature. Bibiji sat her Bhushan examinations alongside Savitri, our eldest sister. They shared course books. Mother went with Savitri to the college in Hoshiarpur to make sure that no one prevented Savitri from attending. It wasn't easy for Bibiji, being an educated woman in the village, and wanting her daughters to be educated in those days. Stones were thrown at her sometimes, and Bapu was rough with her too. But she did everything – cooking and cleaning, sewing and stitching, taking care of us when we were sick. She would say to us, "If I don't do the housework, people will never let their girls be educated. They will say that education spoils girls and ruins women. But girls must be educated. If women are educated, it is not only good for them and their families, it is good for India."'

My aunt uttered the last statement with feeling. It had become her personal crusade; I had heard her express it with fierce passion innumerable times, to domestic workers and tradesmen coming to work in her house, and to neighbours and strangers with whom she entered into conversation. I wanted to tell her that the case was closed, that there had been countless studies across the world, which had confirmed the awesome power of this simple formula: that societies and nations grow richer in a myriad of ways through the advancement of their women.

But she gave me no opportunity to interrupt, and continued: 'Of course, as we grew up, all of us had to contribute to running the household. Savitri and I would help with the domestic chores, and the boys would go out and cut the grass to feed our cows and milk them. I remember your father would often come back from the fields with the cows, singing or whistling. There was a woman in the village who worked for All India Radio. She asked to record him. I think she did record him. He had a beautiful voice...'

She looked at me – she did this sometimes when the conversation turned to my late father – as if to see how much of my father was in me. Then she returned to her recollections, her palms together, right hand on the left hand, resting in her lap.

'In the Bhushan exams Bibiji was the top student and won a prize. She got a book, *The Brihadaranyaka Upanishad* by Swami Dayananda (the founder of the Arya Samaj). Here it is. The original inscribed copy. Bibiji left it for me. I often wonder who I will leave this book for when I die. My children don't seem interested...'

Now I saw the book, with its reddish-brown hard cover. It had been by her side all the time alongside the hardback folder and I had paid no attention to it. She held it easily, flipped it open at random, her eyes running freely over the Hindi script. She passed it over to me. I couldn't read the Hindi, but the spoken title had stirred a memory.

I recalled a wall poster that I had bought to stick on the yellow walls of my room as an undergraduate at Keele University. It had been the kind of contrived act that people on the outside do to exaggerate their 'otherness' and disguise this as uniqueness. The poster had a verse with four simple lines of theology that resonated intuitively, and yet was sufficiently askance to be disconcertingly esoteric to colleagues from Abrahamic faiths in which the centrality of God is invoked loudly, evangelically. I had liked the way the verse ended with the authority of a Hindu scripture, though there was always the fear of being unmasked at not being able to read the original in Sanskrit or Hindi.

Lead us from the unreal to the real,
Lead us from darkness to light,
From death to immortality,
Let there be peace, peace, peace ...

Brihadaranyaka Upanishad, 1.3.28

I handed the book back to my aunt. It was curious how that verse had found me and stayed loyally with me all these years. My aunt took the book back tenderly and held it close. She was quiet for a while, and then put it away by her side.

Then she began again: 'Bibiji taught us all the school subjects up to Matric level. She would study all previous exam papers and teach us accordingly. She was fiercely determined that we do well. She would sit with us and say: "Study, study – become something. Or there is only hunger, poverty and death ahead."

'You know that Bapu's eldest brother, Tara Chand Soni, was an engineer who studied in England in 1910 and returned to work on the building of the Punjab canals? His wife and family were very arrogant. They looked down on us. Many people in the village looked down on us. Bibiji would say to us: "Treat everyone the same – the rich and the poor. Don't ever do what is being done to us." And to the relatives who sneered, I heard her say: "My children too will be graduates one day."

'She didn't see it happen. But look for yourself now, and see how full of fruit her tree is."

It was a similar metaphor to the one that my uncle had used. There was no surprise in this. After all, the family came from agricultural stock. The surprise was to hear my aunt use the imagery of that metaphor again, in a different form because she had said to me earlier, in a different conversation, 'Always remember, son, that the tree that is full of fruit bends low with humility.'

That night, as I reflected on my notes, I noticed that my aunt's account, and my uncle's before her, made no reference to the event of Bibiji's death. Thirty-five years earlier, when I had visited the village of Bajwara, my presence had evoked in the memories of local inhabitants the impact of Bibiji's death on her children. Yet neither Bibiji's surviving son nor daughter had described the day when their world was changed forever.

I decided I would return to the ancestral village with my aunt and raise the dead there.

We telephoned ahead to tell Satpal that we would be coming. He rented and farmed the agricultural land that Bapu had left behind, and kept an eye on the ancestral house.

My aunt had not been back to the village for over 50 years and wanted the driver of our taxi, which we had hired in Delhi, to ask directions. I laughed. My left elbow hung out of the car window as the breeze played with my hair and the landscape talked to me. I found the old tracks hidden behind new buildings and new roads cutting through ancient, sandy flats. The acuity made me giddy with juvenile pleasure.

We stopped the car on the outskirts of the village to weave our way through the alleys to the house. No one recognised us. When Bibiji died in 1946, the demography of Bajwara had been 45 percent 'caste' Hindus – taken to mean essentially the upper three castes, 45 percent upper-class Muslims, and 10 percent Dalits or, as they were known then, 'untouchable' castes. Now, Dalits made up more than 80 percent of the population. The village was essentially a satellite conurbation for unskilled workers serving the industrialising town of Hoshiarpur and providing agricultural labour for farms further away from the town.

The Muslims were all gone. The community from Bajwara had been one of the few that had escaped intact to Pakistan, ushered out safely under the umbrella of goodwill forged between the faiths over centuries. The caste Hindus, educated in the still highly regarded school set up by my distant ancestors, had migrated to cities not just in India but around the world.

My aunt looked around at the mixture of crumbling facades and freshly painted frontages. There was a detached, almost supercilious curiosity painted on her face. It reminded me of her days as a Big Noise. As we turned the corner to walk the final steps to the house, I asked in Punjabi: 'How do you feel? Do you have any emotions?'

'What emotions, Son? Where the trader goes, there goes the trade,' she replied.

I said I didn't understand.

'You just move on in life. I haven't been back since I married,' she added.

I watched her closely. A light, wry, cold smile flickered over her face, momentarily puncturing her composure. Her step had quickened. Satpal had gone ahead and was unshackling a silver lock that held together the pair of shrivelling and warped doors, each about three metres tall and a metre wide.

He pushed the doors open and we walked in. Satpal led the way. I followed, then my aunt. She took four, five steps into the house and stopped. She stood still and silent, her eyes sweeping the barren, dust-free floor.

Each of the steps leading to the upper floor and terrace was about a foot high, two feet deep and four feet wide. Bibiji would have stood there and shouted up at her sleeping brood, rousing them after she had laid out a neat line of tumblers of hot milk on the low bench-wall edging the veranda.

She would have climbed up there in the afternoons, leading the children. It was on the terrace that she fought her fate and escaped into the future. The children were tutored there, as far up as physically possible from the litigious ground that had destroyed the family's harmony and eaten away at its fortunes and ancestral wealth. She had seen that the prosperity of her family, and indeed of India, did not lie in the finite resource of land, subject as this was to the multiplying claims of entitlement from successive generations. The future lay in the limitless capital of education.

I looked out over the verdant fields, the curse of Punjab. It was impossible not to be seduced by the lushness and serenity that lay before us – to penetrate this green veil and recognise the true face of a land that was riddled with centuries of conflict: foreign army against native over dominion, rajah against rajah over glacial waters, subject against ruler over tribute, lessee against *zamindar* over tax, brother against brother over inheritance.

I turned to Satpal. He was younger than me, but looked 10-to-20 years older. The balmy breeze brushing lightly against our skin could not soothe away the premature wrinkles from his face. I asked him about the fields before us, what grew on them, how far the crop stretched, how many yields were possible in a year. He spoke cautiously at first. He had figured out that I was Bapu's eldest grandson through his sons, the eldest carrying the family name. Then slowly he relaxed once he realised that I had no ulterior motives regarding ownership, and contesting my cousin's hold on this land; that my interest lay only in harvesting the stories. We looked far, across half a sweep of a compass. He pointed out orchards and furrowed fields, ancient Soni land and those of others. We spoke of the seasons, of peas and potatoes, mangoes and *moolies*. In the distance, a woman in a loose soiled blue-and-yellow *salwar-kameeze* was walking with a beaker towards a shrine – a small, whitewashed temple set amongst a grove in the fields to the left of our vision.

I asked him what area he was now renting and farming. It was a barely a sliver of the vista before us, about 50-to-60 metres wide, and perhaps 200 metres in length. An incongruous calculation came to mind: two hockey pitches in a line.

My aunt interrupted our conversation.

'Your father stood here.'

I was on the spot where my father had sung an elegy to Bibiji. Before him that day were the fields that had been lost by Bapu in litigation and gambling. With them had gone the money that would have fetched a doctor and medication from Hoshiarpur in the absence of the village doctor. Bibiji had, of course, come up here often, and seen that the deliverance of her children lay not in the furrows of this ephemeral land, but in the fertility of books.

I walked back down the stairs from the terrace with my aunt. The muscles in her face were trembling. She began shuffling forward slowly towards a courtyard veranda that looked onto the small sheltered garden. Her right hand gripped the frame of a door for support. I looked past her. Beyond the *stoep*, about 10-to-12 steps away, by a crumbling wall, was a rose bush. A crimson rose in full bloom was leaning towards us. It was surrounded by a clutch of buds and young, unfolding petals.

My aunt was pointing to the floor a metre from where she stood. Her flaccid arm barely rose to match her words. 'This is where they put Bibiji when they knew she was going to die. She was lying on this floor. Agya, the barber's wife, was sitting next to her. Bibiji begged Agya to intercede on her behalf. She kept saying, "Pray that I may be blessed with another four to five years. My children are too vulnerable – my brood too weak and scattered. I still need to shelter and nurture them." She was groaning and begging. She looked so feeble, so yellow. Then she stopped, and slipped into a coma.'

'We were watching; all of us who were here – all the children. Then Ram Pal came and sat by her. Bibiji rose when she saw him. She came to life, moved towards him. And then she coughed. A splash of phlegm flew from her mouth and landed on the back of Ram's wrist. And then...'

She couldn't continue. I followed my aunt to where she was standing by the rose bush. I had not seen her cry like this before. Her cheeks were streaming with tears, her body quaking with the agitation of a child.

'These emotions in my heart...' she kept saying. 'These emotions in my heart... I can't cope. It is all so vivid after all these years.'

It took her time to stop. She did not want to walk around the house. She wanted to leave, but the images were still stalking her.

'There was a cancer in Bibiji's throat,' she said. 'The poison in there fell on Ram and burnt through his skin. I saw that happen.'

I wanted to ask again about the legacies of that poison. Soon after her passing, Bibiji's favourite son, Ram Pal – the first to graduate – had also died, as if marked by the curse of her final breath. He was murdered for marrying a woman of his choice and left behind a widow from a six-month-old marriage.

Their story had begun away in the foothills of the Himalayas, in the forests of Himachal. He had trained as a forester and been posted to a forest reserve. He had met a teacher from a nearby village, and they had fallen in love. Meanwhile, Bapu had 'promised his hand' to a family with whom he was acquainted. I suspected that a dowry had been part of the negotiations. These events had taken place after Bibiji's death, and Ram had stood up to Bapu to marry the woman of his choice.

Six months after the marriage, he had come home to the village, and agreed to go and see the family who had hoped to marry their daughter to him. Out of courtesy, he had eaten at their house that evening. His body lay on a pyre the next day.

I had been told that his widow, now over 80, was still alive, in good health and living somewhere near Ludhiana. She had remained unmarried all these 57 years and kept her married name, but was not willing to see anyone from the Soni side of the family.

She had found her own way to make peace with her fate, and redeem the death of my uncle. She had devoted her life to the education of girls and women, finally retiring as a principal of a women's college. In the 50 years since my uncle's death, the proportion of girls going to college in India had steadily increased every year. Over 40 percent of the country's graduates were now women, and more than 50 percent of them went on to complete postgraduate degrees. Perhaps that is why she had felt no need to meet. Her story was writ large within these figures.

Everywhere I looked there were stories and stories, and questions within stories. Behind me was the 'outside' kitchen extension that Bibiji had designed and had built in the 1930s. She had planned it – drawing on her own intelligence and the wisdom in her genes from a father who was an engineer in the 19th century – so that the fumes of domesticity would leave swiftly through a draft-inducing pattern of windows and vents.

The latrine was set discreetly in the far corner of the garden. The well was safely walled. It sat in the centre of a triangle, equidistant from inescapable demands: the pots that would sit on the cooking fire, the bathing area behind the kitchen walls, and the spot to which a drink would need to be delivered to a husband tired from the labours of card games. In this geography of chores the rose bush stood as incongruously as a thorn on its stalk, while its stem spoke of pruning and renewal. Who had planted it and how had it survived all these years of neglect?

As my aunt walked out of the house, I told her and Satpal that I wanted to go back up to the open rooftop terrace to which my father had never returned after leaving the village. This time, I looked back towards the village, over the courtyard and the enclosure where the cows had been kept. The walls of the pen had collapsed, and I could see bags of fertilizer that had been piled up by Satpal to force three annual crops from the exhausted soil. The neighbouring houses all looked decrepit. A village with a recorded history going back to the 11th century – and possibly back to Hsuen Tsang's journey through these parts in the seventh century – was dying again. I walked around the terrace, stepping over the clumps of grass and weeds growing in the crevices. Perhaps it was the surprise of these tufts of grass rather than the nudging of ghosts that made me lose my balance. I stumbled, and hovered precariously over a snaking, yawning crack in the terrace, enlarged by the earthquake of 2005 which had devastated parts of eastern Pakistan and north-western India. The house was crumbling, and none of Bibiji's children saw any reason to rescue it from disrepair. Their loathing of this house was visceral. The history it held would be gone soon.

It was time to go to Haridwar.

From Delhi we travelled northeast through the industrial towns and sugar fields of Uttar Pradesh to God's Abode, Haridwar. It is here that the holy waters of the Ganges tumble out of the Himalayas and meet the plains.

The journey took five hours on a single-lane national highway jammed with tractors carrying buyers and sellers to the local markets, inter-state haulage lorries marking the trail of the AIDS epidemic, pilgrimage buses packed with immaculately uniformed school children, stooping pensioners and merry marriage parties, cycle rickshaw peddlers proprietarily hogging the tarmac between their villages, horse carts carrying steel girders, and family cars carrying the ashes of loved ones in the opposite direction to the sea for immersion at a consecrated point in a river that would then carry the remains to an ocean 3 000 miles away.

In that medley and profusion of animals, people and vehicles, regularly combined with the metal carcasses of fatal crashes littering the roadside, I kept asking myself whether the road to Lourdes, or Mecca, was ever like this. Was there anywhere else in the world where the highway to a major sacred site was a single-lane dual carriageway and took half the day's sunlight hours to traverse 200 kilometres? That included time, at regular pit stops, for our driver, Ashok, to carefully shepherd sunbathing flies from inside the car windscreen to the ranks of the thousands of fellow creatures waiting to come back in. In South Africa I had seen a cab driver thwack a fly into a smudge with the brash flourish of a Sowetan so that we could return quickly to the business at hand, and the convivial conversation filling the air. Here, on the road to Haridwar, the issue seemed a whole lot more complicated. Perhaps Ashok's concern – for the fly if not for his passengers – came from his Brahminic nature. Or maybe it was because we were going to the place where a Hindu's final accounts of mortality are held.

Haridwar is essentially a city of pilgrims and pundits. North Indian caste-Hindus, who can afford to, come here to conduct the rituals that serve their recent dead. But Haridwar is not just about private prayers and public *pujas* for a wishful future and an unknown afterlife. Haridwar is also a collection of remarkable libraries. It is here that the expanding branches of family trees are recorded, in scrolls and ledgers that reduce each individual's life to merely two or three entries in a litany of centuries.

We parked on the outskirts of the town. Ashok nervously eased our tiny Maruti past an elephant whose lunch of hay had just been served in the patch of earth, which was the public car park. The elephant's forehead was emblazoned with vermillion motifs. It raised its head to let me take a picture, before sweeping its trunk exploratively past a tea vendor's stall.

We set off on foot in search of our pundit, and entered a surprisingly clean market. The alleys had been washed and were free of litter, the waste channels flowing odourlessly. Sweaters from Himachal, shawls from Kashmir, oils and spices from Tamil Naidu, herbs from Jharkhand, sandalwood rosaries from Karnataka, saris and reams of silks from Varanasi, *dhurries* and cotton sheets from Gujarat, incense and icons from Madhya Pradesh, Punjabi sweets and Hyderabadi savouries, coconuts from Kerala, nuts and dried fruits from Andhra, fresh fruits and vegetables from Uttaranchal, jewellery from Rajasthan and contemporary fashion from Mumbai and Kolkata, scriptures, religious books and comics from the publishing houses of New Delhi, CDs, tapes and DVDs from Bollywood – India's commercial geography was all here, as inevitably as a tourist's urge to spend.

The alleys began to narrow as the market stalls and shops gave way to the final row of houses adjoining the *ghats*. We emerged from a passage to an altogether different scene. There was the river, both banks covered with the steps and platforms of the *ghats*. A peepul tree, 30 metres tall, threw its shade on the corner of the square immediately below. Beneath the generous arms of the tree, a herd of cows grazed on food scraps salvaged from a waste dump alongside a far wall. Pilgrims walked through the square going up and down the steps of the *ghats*. Priests and their attendants sat on the steps to the river and along the walls around the square, waiting for business.

I saw a movement in the tree. A troop of grey monkeys was stalking the parcels of food that had been cast into the river. Their swing across the branches gave some idea of the speed of the racing waters. There was a tap on my shoulder.

'Which village are you from?' It was a young man in his early twenties, in the ubiquitous dark trousers and short-sleeved shirts of urban India. The question contained a silent subsidiary that I had no trouble reading.

'Bajwara.'

'Come, follow me.'

We talked along the way, my aunt revealing to him her maiden name with a pride that explained the urgency with which she often sought to impress my lineage upon me.

He led us through a narrow alley, which opened up to the courtyard of a three-storey house. Earthy ochre paint peeled off to reveal damp brickwork. A number of rooms ran off from the broken paving stones. The doors of the rooms were open and in some, families were huddled around figures not always visible.

'Sonis; from Bajwara.'

Four men were sitting talking on two low benches outside an empty room. One came forward. 'Come,' he said. 'Welcome.'

The custodian of our family's history – the one man on Earth with more information in his possession in this respect than any other – was dressed like one of millions of Indians: dark trousers, light short sleeved shirt, and loose plastic sandals. A young man sitting alone moved across to join us. He was about 19 and had a limp, which was made more pronounced by the uneven ground that was buckled by the roots of an old peepul tree. He settled himself quietly by his father's side. I struggled to read his expression. Boredom, detachment and basic human curiosity lurked behind a sombre air of apprenticeship.

I wondered what the encounter would be like if he and my daughters were ever to meet. After my passing they would have to come here to keep the forest of ancestry fresh. It brought to mind a conversation with a Nigerian friend, Chief Kanu, under the evening shade of a flame tree in Abuja. Our self-deprecating laughter about the passage of youth had led to a discussion on mortality and migration, and he had suddenly asked with consternation, 'Who will bury you when you are dead?'

I had struggled to construct a picture of my daughters coming to record my name in the family annals. It was unimaginable; impossible to place myself and look from that side of the final curtain, just as it is to see through that blind from this side. But within this tremulous opacity I also felt a sense of calm in knowing that they, or someone, would come, and that, if my daughters came, they would walk here with an élan rooted in the singularity of their own spirit, suffusing whatever facets of ethnicity and nationality they chose to wear. The trajectory of their life's journey that would bring them here would be as mysterious and unpredictable as mine had been, but I could see the curiosity and sharpness of their minds elaborating arcs of identity between the present and the past.

'So?' asked the pundit.

'I'm researching my grandmother's life,' I said. 'Her name was Lakshmi Devi Soni.'

'We follow the heads of families; the male descendants. The record of her life would have begun in another family. She would only feature in our records after her marriage to your grandfather.'

'I understand that. I want to know if you have a precise date for when she died. I haven't been able to find that anywhere.'

'Let's see. Tell me, whose son are you? And your grandfather?'

'My father was Rajinder Pal Soni. He died on 7 August 1989. His father was Amar Chand Soni.'

He went to the back of the room, and stood before a stack of scrolls and ledgers that reached from the floor to the height of a door. He brought down a tome, with the certainty of a pharmacist picking a particular vial off a set of shelves.

He struggled to open the book, lifting a portion as deep as two volumes of the Oxford Dictionary. The yellow pages were about a foot and half wide, three feet long. He began to flick heavily through the pages. I wanted to seize the book from him, but the unreadable Urdu and Hindi script mocked my intent. A regret that had plagued me for years came to mind again: I wished that somewhere along my life's journey I had summoned the discipline to learn the Devanagari Hindi script.

He found an entry and turned to me. 'Yes I have it here. One of his brothers came to look at these records and told us of your father's death.' Then he stopped and looked directly at me. Reproach flared in his eyes. 'But you haven't conducted the *puja* for your father's death yet.'

'We took his ashes to Rishikesh to the Sivananda Ashram, up the river from here. His guru, Swami Chidanandji, did the ceremony himself. We didn't feel the need to do it here.'

'It is good that his guru conducted the prayers. But who will maintain these records if you don't honour these traditions that are as old as the river itself?' he asked.

I wanted to say that I found his hyperbole unnecessary, but instead I responded, 'We'll do the *puja*. But can we please look at the records?'

His concern was to record new information first. The value of the records and his ancestral profession lay in maintaining their integrity and vitality. He wanted to know about each individual of my generation and whether they were alive or dead, married, childless or had children. I could see that each branch, each character needed to be revisited whenever a source of information came into his presence.

'Elizabeth Sarah,' I said, giving him my wife's name.

'Like the queen?' he asked.

'Yes. And my daughters are Radha Maud and Aditi Laxmi.'

He struggled with the Maud, but wrote the Hindi words quickly and neatly, adding my daughters' birthdates alongside their names. Then he began to work his way back through the pages.

'Your grandmother, Lakshmi Devi Soni, died on 23 April 1946 in Bajwara. Your father brought her ashes here; he came with his father and a brother who was two years old. Your grandmother's ashes were placed in the Mother Ganges on 29 April 1946. Your father performed the *puja*. Here is the entry in his handwriting.'

They would have come by *tonga*, over three days, setting out the day after Bibiji's cremation. My father would have been 16 when he wrote that entry. His writing hadn't changed with adulthood. I recognised the slanting scribble: tiny crowded letters, with the sentences rising and ending at a higher point than where they had started on the page, like the buoyancy of his laugh after a Kabir poem. Postcards and letters in that script had reached me wherever I had lived around the world. Now they had leapt from a desolate past to enter an inchoate future.

We paused. The pundit insisted we conduct the *puja* for my father by the sacred waters before he lodged its enactment in the ledger. We made our way to the Ganges. A lissom young man, an eel in human form, was dipping in and out of the racing currents. I saw him open his eyes wide as he submerged his head, scouring the riverbed for sanctified coins.

I felt no surge of piety as the river washed around my knees. The pundit settled himself on the concrete steps two to three metres away and began reciting mantras in Sanskrit. Occasionally, he would insert my father's name in a verse, and then stop to issue instructions. I would reach back to fetch blobs of freshly kneaded flour, grains of puffed rice, coconuts and beakers filled with the river's water to pour back into the flow. Only my father's ashes were missing, having already passed this way many years ago.

Memories of the past took me further upstream. I wondered what state my father would have been in when he and Bapu made their way here from Punjab across the parched, famine stricken land nearly 60 years ago. Of Bibiji's nine living children at the time of her death, he was the fifth. What sense had he made of a fate that placed this responsibility on him? I looked down at the concrete steps. There would have been rocks then, buffeted by fierce, racing currents. What simple offerings of food and flowers would he have placed in the swirling eddies of the undammed river of those days?

The priest broke into my thoughts. He required me to cup my hands, scoop the racing waters and drink them to his intonations. I readied myself by walking deeper into the river up to waist height, turned my back to him, and my face towards the far bank. Each time the pundit called out his instructions, I bent into the Ganges, brought out the water and let it slip through my fingers before a drop could cross my lips. The deceit felt delicious.

Yet, as we walked back up the alley, I realised that I had not emerged untouched by the river's embrace. I silently saluted the peepul tree in the courtyard of the pundit's chambers, which had smelt the perfume of Bibiji's ashes and given shade to my father's broken, young heart. I looked at the pundit differently, more tolerant of his financial avarice. If we are blessed, then death visits our families infrequently, spacing these rituals apart by generations. I was less begrudging of him than I had felt initially when he had asked for $60 for his services, in a country where nearly 300,000,000 people lived on less than a dollar a day.

I recalled hearing, as a child in Mombasa, of an enduring tradition, of a lineage of pundits who lived by a river in northern India, who held the timeless records of my family. That knowledge had been a source of comfort when I had drifted away from the search for Bibiji. I had taken solace in the thought that, if I failed to write about her, at least someone, somewhere, had noted her passage, even if the story of her sacrifice and vision remained buried.

We left the pundit wealthier, possibly wiser. In the book on the Sonis of Bajwara, I had insisted on inserting the names of my daughters as my heirs. My aunt had intervened energetically, quoting Indian laws that enshrined the equality of female and male heirs. At first, the pundit had argued with us, but then he had conceded quickly; he could read the currents of history. The changes which Bibiji had envisioned, for the role of Indian women in family and society were now beyond dispute in the country, and more pertinently in the class of people with whom the pundit and his descendants needed to do business.

I signed the entry attesting to my visit. As he closed the book, the pundit handed me his business card: a whirlpool of bobbing blue script on a larger than usual canvas. I returned to my hotel room and put the card into my bag with a niggling hint of self-reproach. There was a sense of accomplishment in discovering the precise date of Bibiji's death, and a strange comfort in learning that my father had carried her ashes for three days, meditating on her life as he came of age and travelled shoulder to shoulder with Bapu. But I felt disappointed with myself for allowing my respect for him as a chronicler to override the mumbo-jumbo that had followed. I was troubled by the silence with which I had met the pundit's final statements, his bizarre theological claim of damnation if the sacraments by the river were not performed to send the departed soul propitiously on its onward journey.

I went for a walk alone by the river later that evening, back down to the *ghats*, at the time of the evening *aarti*. The prayer bells were ringing and a million candles floated on the water, in batches released almost simultaneously by different groups of worshippers; slowly moving carpets made of tiny, bright, orange-red flames, ablaze and riding tranquilly on an ambrosial river. If there was a meaning to the rituals of Haridwar it was here: that the fire of the spirit shines brightest in the darkness, with a radiance and beauty that lingers forever in the mind. The flames lit up a tenet that my father had always insisted on: 'Use your mind; don't ever fall prey to the superstitious nonsense of pundits.'

He always used the word '*buddhi*' for the mind, which resonated with the Buddha's insistence on never letting go of reason and direct experience, especially when on a spiritual quest. That had come from Bibiji – not from her familiarity with Buddhism, but from virtually identical teachings in the Arya Samaj. In all the stories that I had unearthed about her, there wasn't one where she had succumbed to *pujas* and pundits. Even as she lay dying she had asked, not for a Brahmin priest to invoke the gods on her behalf, to twist the threads of fate by liturgical bribery, but had sought instead the agency of the barber's wife, the midwife who had helped usher her children into life. Her abiding refrain to her children had been, 'Study – educate yourselves' .

I knew now why I hadn't sipped the waters of the river in the morning. Any fool could see that the flow of the water was weak, diminished by agricultural diversion and susceptible to pollution. And as I stood in the river, I had remembered an earlier visit upriver to a gorge near Rishikesh where the rocks by the riverbanks had stunk of faeces.

I sat on the steps and reflected on the mixture of emotions and motives that the river stirred in me, as I watched men dressed in deathly white saying final prayers, and families dressed in bright colours drinking in the unadulterated pleasure of being in the presence of living, glacial water. I smiled at a passing family; parents with two girls and a boy, all between the ages of four and eight, and wide-eyed at the spectacle of fire dancing on water. There was something particularly Indian, yet poignantly universal about this nuclear unit; the humdrum neatness of the man's polyester clothes, the subtle elegance of the woman's silk sari, the older girl in a floral cotton dress walking by her mother's side and holding the hand of the youngest child in his bright red shirt, while the other girl, in a pretty turquoise dress, sidled up to her father. The family was typical of the millions of Hindus who come every year to Haridwar not to perform obligatory *pujas*, but as pilgrim-tourists, drawn by the city's mythological reputation as the 'Gateway to the Gods' and the natural beauty of its location in the Shivalik foothills. And being in Haridwar, it was impossible not to ask who among them would go across first? Whose destiny would it be to relate the family's history?

I rose and walked towards the darker end of the *ghat*, where three bearded men with long matted hair wearing soiled orange sadhu robes were sitting looking out at the river. There was a halo of wispy smoke over them. I took in the aroma as I walked past, and caught an unmistakable blast of Peter Tosh's 'holy herb'. As ever in India, there was always another way to cut one's ties to ancestral land and roam the world as a free spirit that knows no boundary; only the joy of flight and the certainty of returning.

A few months later, I sat writing in my study in Birmingham in the early morning. It was mid-April and the magnolia tree was in bloom in the garden. It had always struck me as an unusual tree, bursting into flower seemingly unseasonally, before breaking profusely into leaf. Every summer that I had sat in its shade, I had felt a tinge of sadness, that this magnificent abundance of green and life, with leaves that were virtually indestructible, never saw the flowers that had provided the seed for their very existence. That morning as I lingered on the extravagant white and pink blossom, an orb of bulbous candles saluting the warmth of the sun, I thought of Bibiji – a woman before her time, a flower sacrificing itself to signal the coming of spring.

Then my young daughters – Radha was five and Aditi three and half at the time – came into my study, which was lined with books and files on beech-wood shelves. Gradually, they settled in to play on the wooden floor, occasionally rising to rifle through drawers, upturning and rearranging piles of books and papers. It struck me how natural this habitat was for them. They knew where the paper and pens were stored, the switches to the table lamp, computer and printer, the grip of fingers on a mouse.

When they left my study, I noticed that one had drawn a sketch of stick figures signed with a loving message, and the other had written a short story. I savoured their creations before filing them away a few days later in their respective scrapbooks, which contained small, incidental slices of daily life; stories of our shared time and encoded clues to their individual destinies. This urge to salvage pieces of history and mementoes of the present, had grown, unconsciously at first, from tracing Bibiji's brief life, from contemplating my father's short life, and then, more deliberately, as I sought to understand the forces that have shaped me.

The journey to find her, and through her myself, had taught me that this impulse to discover the past and define oneself was not just a sentimental enterprise, or a matter of tailoring the labels of identity more comfortably, though those superficial motives are present too. Everyone passes on, and nations too. All the labels are transient. That is an absolute certainty of the human condition. But values and visions remain, even if they are invisible to those who are shaped by their force in subsequent generations. If I had found one truth on this journey, it was that the meaning and purpose that an anonymous woman had brought to her life, and the spirit with which she had lived, remained eternal. It was these instincts of wisdom and innate power, latent within the etchings, writings and conversations of my daughters – Bibiji's great-granddaughters – that I wished to preserve, not for them but for their grandchildren.

Several days after this, at the end of a working day as I tidied up my study, restoring everything to its rightful place after yet another visit from the girls, I found an item in a bookcase that I had set aside for them. It was a business card and was printed on two sides; Hindi on one, English on the other. The whirly blue script was composed with poor ink and printed on coarse paper, which made for a smudgy, antiquated impression. Either the card had been saved there by the girls, guided by a light beyond their ken, or had slipped into their treasures serendipitously. Both thoughts were equally intriguing.

I studied the card again, having paid little notice to it when it had been handed to me many months earlier in India. It read:

salutations
to the Goddess Ganges

The Holy Ganges at Haridwar
Family Priests & Keepers of Family Records
The Son and Grandson of Ram Pratapji
Pundits Sita-Ram and Radha-Shyam

ADDRESS: TULSIDAS HAVELI, PASS KUSHA GHAT,
HARIDWAR.

I smiled. It was an invitation to enter history, from where my ashes would flow.

Glossary

aarti	a Hindu ritual of worship in which the devotee lights a candle or a wick soaked in ghee (clarified butter), stands facing the altar or sanctum, and sings a traditional devotional hymn. These prayers are offered to the deity of personal choice, or when performed in a temple, to the deities to which the temple is dedicated
Angrez sahibs	Englishmen
Arya Samaj	a reformist Hindu movement founded in 1875 by Swami Dayananda Sarasvati, theologically based on the primacy of the Vedas, the earliest Hindu Scriptures. Though the organisation was first estalbished in Bombay and its founder was from Gujarat, the Arya Samaj developed its strongest following in Punjab where it played a significant role in shaping social and political ideas, espcially on gender equality and Indian nationalism
atta	wholewheat flour used to make most Indian flatbreads, such as chapati, roti, naan and puri

balushahi	a traditional Indian sweatmeat made from maida flour (finely refined and bleached wheat flour, similar to cake flour), sugar and ghee. Balushahi are crispy outside and smooth and soft inside, and once fried are dipped in syrup
barfi	soft milk-based fudge, traditionally made with *khoya* or *mawa* (dried evaporated milk) and sugar. Barfi can be plain or flavoured with cardamom or desiccated coconut, and nuts – typically, pistachio and almonds
bhajan	Hindu devotional song
bhindi	Okra or ladies' fingers
bua	father's sister
buddhi	intelligence, wisdom; a discerning mind
chacha	father's younger brother
chachi	father's younger brother's wife
chapati	an unleavened flatbread (also known as roti) made of wholewheat flour and water, and cooked on a *tava*, a flat or convex frying pan traditionally made of cast iron
charpoy	a bed consisting of a wooden frame strung with interlaced rope to form a webbed base. Traditionally the user would lie directly on top of the ropes without an intervening mattress
chunni	another word for *dupatta*, a scarf-like length of material can be used in two ways: to cover the head, or arranged symmetrical across the neck and chest and thrown back around the shoulders, worn by women typically with a *salwar-kameeze*
dahdah	father's father (paternal grandfather)
dahdee	father's mother (paternal grandmother)

desi	local, native, indigenous. The term is increasingly used colloquailly to mean someone or something from India, including the diaspora
dhabha	a roadside restaurant especially common in Punjab, selling freshly cooked local food and usually located next to highways and bus ranks, and on the outskirts of cities, towns, and villages
dharmic (dharma)	a key concept of Hinduism meaning the 'right way of living', or the 'path of righteousness'
dhurrie	a thick, flat rug or mat traditionally made from coarse, woven cotton, and used as a floor-covering
fakir	a Hindu or Muslim religious ascetic who lives only on alms
farz	duty, obligation
filmi	of, or related to, the Mumbai film industry, especially popular Bollywood film music
foofad	father's sister's husband
Gayatri Mantra	an ancient Sanskrit Vedic mantra popularised in North India by the Arya Samaj. For some, the Gayatri Mantra is not just a prayer and means of worship, but also an object of worship in itself
ghat	a set of steps leading down to a body of water (a lake or a river) and particularly to a holy river. Also in some cases a place by the edge of the river where cremations occur
gilli-danda	a game played by two individuals or teams of undefined size, involving two sticks, one small (gilli) and the other long (danda). Crudely, the object is to hit the smaller one with the longer,

	and propel the *gilli* as far as possible without the opposing player or team catching it as it travels through the air
gurudwara	a Sikh temple
haveli	a private mansion or a large house, sometimes with historical and architectural significance
hukam	decree, order, command, sanction
izzat	the concept of honour, reputation, respect, or prestige prevalent in the culture of Punjab
Jaat	a social group. The term is loosely applied in colloquial Punjabi and can refer to a clan, caste or a community with a particular religious affiliation
jalebis	sweetmeats made by deep-frying coils of batter in pretzel or circular shapes, which are then soaked in syrup
Jallianwala Bagh	a public garden in Amritsar in Punjab of seminal signifiance to the Independence Movement. The park contains a memorial commemorating the Jallianwala Bagh massacre of civilians by British forces on 13 April, 1919
ji ha	yes sir
karela	bitter gourd (or bitter melon). Karelas sold in a market are usually the size of medium sized cucumbers, green in colour, with wrinkled warty ridges running length wise
khaddar	a hand-loomed cotton fabric of plain weave
kheer	a rice pudding, often flavoured with cardamom, raisins, saffron, pistachios and/or almonds
khitchri / khichdi	a dish made from a mixture of rice and lentils, and often lightly spiced. The term is also used

	methaphorically to mean a hotchpotch of issues
kurta	a loose, collarless shirt, usually extending at least to the knees. Women wear a *kurta* with a *salwar*, and men with pyjamas
laddoos	a round, ball-shaped sweet, made from gram flour, ghee, milk and sugar, and flavoured with cardamon, saffron and nuts (pistachios or almonds)
lassi	a sweet or salty drink made from yogurt and water
maa ki daal	a popular Punjabi dish, made from black lentils
mahmah	mother's brother
mahmi	mother's brother's wife
mahsi	mother's sister
masad	mother's sister's husband
masti	mischief
moolie	long, white radish, shaped like a carrot, and about twice the size
mzee	an elder, a respected person, a dignified man. The term is often used as title of respect in Swahili
nana	mother's father (maternal grandfather)
nani	mother's mother (maternal grandmother)
paisa	a monetary unit equal to one hundredth of a rupee
pir	a Sufi saint or holy man; a spiritual teacher
puja	a prayer ceremony performed either at home or in the *mandir* (temple), often involving

singing the *aarti*. The term can also be used to suggest an act of reverence to aspects of the divine through meditation and invocation

Ramayana — The Ramayana – the Story of Rama – is one of two epic Hindu poems (the other is the Mahabharata). It is one of India's oldest and most popular stories, and embodies the Hindu concept of dharma: principles of duty and righteousness - behaving dutifully, correctly and righteously through life. Diwali, 'the festival of light' marks a momentous event in this story

saag — a green, leaf-based dish usually made from spinach and mustard leaf, especially popular in Punjab

sadhu — a holy man, sage or ascetic

saghan (or shagun) — a gift (usually of money, almonds or sweets) given on special occasions such as an engagement or marriage

salwar-kameeze — a type of suit usually consisting of loose, pleated trousers tapering to a tight fit around the ankles (*salwar*), and a long shirt (*kameeze*). Both women and men can wear a *salwar-kameeze*, though the style of the suit will vary according to gender

seedha — straight; also used ironically, to suggest a slightly stupid person

shabash — well done! (usually said as an exclamation)

thaya — father's elder brother

thayi — father's elder brother's wife

tonga — a light horse-drawn, two-wheeled vehicle, similar to a horse and cart wallah   a person associated with, or engaged in, a particular business eg rickshaw-*wallah*, or from a particular place eg Mumbai-*wallah*

zamindar   a landowner, especially one who leases his land to tenant farmers

About the author

RAJAN SONI is a humanitarian and international development consultant with more than 30 years' experience across Africa, Europe, Asia and the Pacific, the Americas and the Caribbean.

He holds a combined BA honours degree in Maths and Economics from Keele University, as well as an MSc in Organisational Development from Sheffield Business School, both in the UK. Most recently he has been awarded an MA in Creative Writing from The University of the Witwatersrand, in South Africa.

He sees himself as an inhabitant of the world; living, working, and wandering through more than 60 countries in five continents.

He has been travelling since birth. His first wide-eyed journey was from Mombasa to Zanzibar in the arms of his mother. He has been itinerant ever since. Through his life he has been fortunate to meet three people who recognized him wholly in this time. All three were blind.

The first, a retired Scottish sea merchant, was sitting on an adjoining table in a Chinese Café, drinking ginseng tea. He turned, tapped a shoulder and said: 'Sorry sir, I have been eavesdropping on your conversation. I've travelled the world but can't figure out where you are from. What nationality are you?'

The second was a scholarly man with a tapping white stick on a train meandering slowly through the Snake Pass in the Peak District of South Yorkshire. At the end of an hour's conversation, he said: 'Good talking to you sir, but before I get off, can you tell me which country you are from?'

The third was in a workshop in a nondescript conference room, in a forgotten corner of the world. A woman blinking sightlessly pointed diagonally across the circle of chairs and said: 'I can't place that man speaking from over there. At first I thought I heard an African speaking. But then I thought I heard an Indian accent. But I have listened closely to what he's been saying, and I just don't know. Sir, can I please feel your hair?'

Rajan Soni now lives happily in his skin, with greying hair and an eclectic mix of contradictions. He is based in London to be close to his daughters. He resides on a quiet street in South East London, an hour away from the busiest airport in the world. He works as a consultant in international development, and likes to read, write, and travel with his daughters.

About the Unisa Flame Series editors

ALAN WEINBERG is the editor and author of several works including *The Unfamiliar Shelley*, vol. 2 forthcoming. In 2011, he became Unisa's first A-rated Humanities researcher. He has wide experience in critical studies and textual scholarship. He is an emeritus professor actively engaged in advancing research capacity within South Africa and in promoting the Unisa Press Commissioning Programme. He is a member of the Academy of Science in South Africa (ASSAF), and has served as a panellist on the NRF Executive Evaluation Committee.

PROF. KEYAN TOMASELLI has published extensively in the field of Cultural and Media Studies, covering film studies, public health communication, and cultural tourism and indigeneity. He is the editor of *Critical Arts: South-North Cultural and Media Studies* and founding editor of *Journal of African Cinemas*. He served on the Academy of Science in South Africa's Consensus Panel on the Humanities and is a Fellow of the University of KwaZulu-Natal and of the International Communicology Institute. Prof. Tomaselli is also a satirical columnist for a number of university magazines.